With a shake of his head, Leo pulled the blanket around his shoulders. "At first I just figured I'd given myself the heebie-jeebies."

Heebie-jeebies? Cole bit his tongue.

"I could swear I felt someone watching me. That was Monday. Tuesday night there was a suspicious car in the parking lot when I got home."

Okay, that definitely sounded like heebie-jeebies. Maybe he'd just gotten a little too close to the paranormal world and it had freaked him out. Cole inclined his head toward Niamh.

She ruffled her feathers but made for the kitchen without complaint. Cole heard the scrape of talons on the counter as she picked up the cloth bag of sweets he kept for emergencies—though this particular emergency he had not foreseen.

To Leo, Cole prompted, "Go on."

Welcome to

DREAMSPUN BEYOND

Dear Reader,

Everyone knows love brings a touch of magic to your life. And the presence of paranormal thrills can make a romance that much more exciting. Dreamspun Beyond selections tell stories of love featuring your favorite shifters, vampires, wizards, and more falling in love amid paranormal twists. Stories that make your breath catch and your imagination soar.

In the pages of these imaginative love stories, readers can escape to a contemporary world flavored with a touch of the paranormal where love conquers all despite challenges, the thrill of a first kiss sweeps you away, and your heart pounds at the sight of the one you love. When you put it all together, you discover romance in its truest form, no matter what world you come from.

Love sees no difference.

Elizabeth North

Executive Director
Dreamspinner Press

Ashlyn Kane

HEX AND CANDY

DREAMSPUN BEYOND

PUBLISHED BY

DREAMSPINNER
PRESS

Published by
DREAMSPINNER PRESS

5032 Capital Circle SW, Suite 2, PMB# 279,
Tallahassee, FL 32305-7886 USA
www.dreamspinnerpress.com

This is a work of fiction. Names, characters, places, and incidents either
are the product of author imagination or are used fictitiously, and any
resemblance to actual persons, living or dead, business establishments,
events, or locales is entirely coincidental.

Hex and Candy
© 2018 Ashlyn Kane.
Editorial Development by Sue Brown-Moore.

Cover Art
© 2018 Aaron Anderson.
aaronbydesign55@gmail.com
Cover content is for illustrative purposes only and any person depicted
on the cover is a model.

Paperback ISBN: 978-1-64108-105-4
Digital ISBN: 978-1-64080-739-6
Library of Congress Control Number: 2018940826
Paperback published August 2018
v. 1.0

Printed in the United States of America
∞
This paper meets the requirements of
ANSI/NISO Z39.48-1992 (Permanence of Paper).

ASHLYN KANE is a Canadian former expat and current hockey fan. She is a writer, editor, handyperson, dog mom, and friend—sometimes all at once.

On any given day, she can usually be found walking her ninety-pound baby chocolate lapdog, Indy, or holed up in her office avoiding housework. She has a deep and abiding love of romance-novel tropes, a habit of dropping too many f-bombs, and—fortunately—a very forgiving family.

Twitter: @ashlynkane
Facebook: www.facebook.com/ashlyn.kane.94
Website: Ashlynkane.ca

By Ashlyn Kane

DREAMSPUN BEYOND
STRANGE BEDFELLOWS
#26 – Hex and Candy

DREAMSPUN DESIRES
#59 – His Leading Man

Published by **DREAMSPINNER PRESS**
www.dreamspinnerpress.com

For the usual cast of cheerleaders: Amanda, Amy, Brandon, Kate, and Laura.
I couldn't have done it without you.

Chapter One

"COLE, I need three pounds of lemon drops!"

Cole Alpin paused with his finger just above the surface of his tablet and considered the frequency at which one might vibrate if one consumed three pounds of lemon drops. Then he tapped in his sugar order, set the tablet on the shelf, and poked his head around the corner into the storefront. "Three pounds?"

Amy flipped her planner closed and gave him a frazzled smile. "It's for a baby shower. Mom-to-be wants a candy bar with everything lemon."

How many people were attending this shindig if she needed three pounds of one kind of candy? "When do you need it?" He gestured toward the lemon drop bin, which held only a few sad handfuls. "Back-to-school cleaned me out, but I can do up a batch tonight if she's set on those."

"I was kidding. Let's do the usual assorted mix with a lemon theme."

Thank God. Cole had an urgent date with his couch and this week's *Dancing with the Stars*. "Done." He made a note on the pad beside the register. Then he frowned. "Are you okay?" She was a little green under her perfect makeup.

"I just had a lunch meeting with someone suffering from acute morning sickness. Morning sickness that didn't stay in the morning."

Amy was a sympathetic vomiter. "Why…?" Cole started and then decided it didn't matter. He opened the jar of special mints next to the register and used the tongs to pull one out. "Never mind. Here."

But then his curiosity got the better of him again and he blurted out, "Okay, no, seriously. Why would she ask for a lunch meeting?"

Amy popped the mint in her mouth and shrugged. "Hope springs eternal?" She shook her head. Her color was already returning to normal, and she stood a little straighter. "I swear to God these candies are magic."

"Secret recipe," Cole said, projecting the very image of innocence.

"Well, your secret recipe has saved my day. I have a two o'clock at the golf course about a fundraiser dinner." She stood on tiptoe, and he leaned over the counter so she could kiss his cheek. "Can I pick up on Friday?"

The bell above the door jingled, and Cole looked up automatically and forgot how to breathe with his mouth closed.

Amy followed his gaze over her shoulder, then turned back toward him, smirking. "Friday, Cole. I'll call and remind you."

She collected her planner from the countertop and sashayed out, turning as she did to give the newcomer a once-over from another angle. *Wow*, she mouthed at Cole.

The door closed behind her.

Cole swallowed hard.

"Uh, hi." The guy who'd entered was probably six two, with shoulders like Atlas and a physique that suggested he'd never even looked at a piece of candy. "Are you Cole?"

And he was asking for Cole by name. Was Cole dreaming? Had he slipped into an alternate dimension? "Yeah, yes, hi. I'm Cole." Belatedly he stuck out his hand to shake.

"Leon," said the absolutely radiant human being. Cole would have sworn the sunlight coming in the shop window glinted off his blinding smile. His warm hand practically dwarfed Cole's, and Cole wasn't exactly dainty. "Um, Leo. I'm—a friend of mine told me you might be able to help me?"

Cole owed this friend a fruit basket. "I will do my best to be your sugar daddy." His eyes went wide and his face went hot and he could *feel* himself going blotchy all over. "I mean! Uh. I sell candy, obviously. And I will sell some. To you."

A hint of strain crept into Leo's smile. "Actually I didn't come here to buy candy."

Cole blinked. He didn't sell anything other than candy. "Okay?"

Leo let out a miserable sound. "I've got this—problem." He scrunched up his face. "Like a... man problem."

What did that mean? Was he looking for a hit man or a pimp? "I'm sorry to hear that?" Cole offered, having no earthly idea what else to say. He could offer himself up as a sacrifice, maybe, but that seemed a little forward.

He didn't think a guy who looked like Leo really needed that kind of help from him anyway.

"Or not exactly a man problem," Leo continued. His ears had started to turn red. "More of a, um, performance issue?"

Oh *wow*, no wonder he looked uncomfortable. "That sucks, man, but you really need to see a doctor about that. I just make candy." Sure, some of them had… extramundane properties, but they'd only treat a symptom, not a cause. Erectile dysfunction was no joke, especially at Leo's age. He should have that looked at.

Leo groaned and slumped onto one of the stools at the fifties-style counter, nearly dislodging a glass jar of jawbreakers with his forearm. He put his head in his hands and muttered something indecipherable at his elbows.

This guy was not having a great day. Cole grabbed the jar of bubble pops and used the tongs to pull one out. "Sorry, I didn't quite catch that."

Leo lifted his head. He was even more beautiful close up, and he smelled good, like citrus and lavender.

Cole swallowed hard again. "Lollipop?"

Leo took it with a sigh and pulled off the wrapper.

Cole realized his mistake when Leo shoved the thing in his mouth and then stuffed it inside his cheek. He needed to think about… burning sugar or something. And not the flash of pink tongue curling around the end of the bubble pop stick.

Yeah, good luck with that. With great concentration, Cole replaced the lid on the jar.

There was a sucking noise—Cole almost died—and then a surprised-sounding hum of satisfaction, which was worse.

Then Leo muttered, "Victoria better be right about this, I swear to God. I feel like an idiot."

Hey, look at that—they already had something in common! They should get married. Cole could totally work with Leo's issue, whatever it was. But before he could open his mouth and put his foot in it, Leo lifted his head and looked him in the eye.

"I don't need a doctor. I need a holistic cursebreaker."

FOR a few seconds all Cole could do was stare at him. Not that it was a hardship. *Holistic cursebreaker*, he'd said. Well, now that Cole knew to turn his power on and look with more than just his eyes—now that Leo's damnably handsome face wasn't distracting him— he *could* sense the threads of some kind of spell: the vibrant green threads of it bound his lips and throat and hands, and maybe more that Cole couldn't see with the counter in the way.

"Boy did you piss someone off," he said before he could help himself. "What's the damage?" He could take a guess, but it would be easier if Leo told him.

Leo seemed to wilt with relief. "You don't think I'm nuts?"

"Please." Cole's family were adepts going back generations. "I've known you for like thirty seconds. But witchcraft, yeah, that's real, and so's the curse you're under."

"And you can undo it?"

That was trickier. "Sometimes. But not during regular business hours. I don't charge for that stuff. Gets too complicated on my taxes."

"I can come back?" Leo offered. "What time do you close? I could meet you here." Apparently he was desperate.

Special candies aside, Cole didn't keep metaphysical tools in the store. "Better idea." He tore a page from his memo book and scrawled his address on the back. "Meet me here. Six o'clock. Bring a pizza or something, this could take a while, and it's hungry work."

Leo took the paper. "So you'll help?"

As if Cole was going to let this hottie go around cursed for the rest of his life. Besides, he could always use the good karma. "I'll help."

When Leo left, it was quarter to four. That gave Cole fifteen minutes to do some research before Danielle came in for the closing shift. He grabbed his phone and hit speed dial.

"Cole! Slow day today?"

"Well, not anymore." He plopped himself on the barstool behind the counter and spun so he had a clear view of the door in case a customer came in. He was about due for an influx of kids needing their after-school sugar rush. "Have you had anyone interesting in the shop lately?"

"Oh, so it's a business call." There was a soft thump as, presumably, Kate sat in the overstuffed rolling armchair behind the desk in her yarn-cum-magic shop across town. Phoenix Fibre carried all kinds of magical paraphernalia, but only if you knew how to look for it. If anyone were shopping around for curse items locally, she'd know. "Why do you ask?"

Cole took a slow breath and attempted to clear all inflection from his voice. "A guy came in today," he began.

He didn't fool her for a hot second. "Uh-huh. On a scale of one to ten, how bad do you want to fuck him?"

"Fourteen," Cole answered promptly. He didn't have time to equivocate, and Kate was his cousin and knew him better than anyone. He wouldn't fool her anyway. "But that's not the point. He's got a curse. A nasty one, from the look of it. Any idea who could have done it?"

"Haven't had anybody new in," Kate said. "Not the witchy type, anyway, just your generic crafty sorts. What kind of mojo are we talking?"

Cole was prone to catastrophizing and didn't want to speculate. "I don't know yet. Keep me posted?"

"I will if you will."

A handful of kids trickled in, the bell above the door jingling merrily. "Promise," Cole said and hung up the phone.

Chapter Two

LEO parked under a huge oak tree on a quiet residential street lined with small but well-kept Victorian bungalows, each in a different color. Number 4 was pink with pristine white gingerbread trim. For a second Leo just stared at it and wondered how he'd gotten here. Three months ago he didn't know witches existed. Now he was bringing one pizza.

He hoped Cole liked pineapple.

He hoped Cole wasn't secretly a serial killer who was going to push him into an oven and bake him.

Aside from being pink, Cole's house looked like all the others on the street. It didn't seem particularly *witchy*. Except—was that a fairy circle in the lawn? Was that a real thing? And were those *bones* hanging from that wind chime under the willow?

This was a bad idea. Leo could live with the curse.

Before he could turn around, though, the front door opened and Cole smiled at him. "Good, you're here. I'm starving."

He didn't look like he was about to throw Leo in the oven, but he *was* making serious heart eyes at the pizza box. Between that and his T-shirt—it sported two bananas and the slogan *you're so appealing*—Leo was disarmed. "No cursebreaking on an empty stomach?"

"No anything on an empty stomach. I get hangry. No one needs to deal with that." Cole stood to one side and gestured Leo into the house. "Come on in."

Well, into the lion's den. Maybe.

The house looked normal on the inside too. Nice hardwood floors, framed photographs on the walls. Sure, there was a broom leaning against the wall by the front door, but that was probably just coincidence, right? Cole tidying up before entertaining a client?

Dealing with the paranormal was a lot easier when Leo just had to eat a lot of red meat and leafy greens.

Cole took the pizza and led the way deeper into the house, the lights coming on as he walked, illuminating his path. Leo screwed his courage to the sticking place and followed, casting around for any kind of opening conversational gambit. *So, how long have you been a witch* seemed like it might be insensitive.

Fortunately Cole took the problem out of his hands. "So, how long have you been playing on our side of the fence?"

Maybe it wasn't so insensitive. Or maybe Cole was just blunter than a rubber mallet. "I met Roman at the beginning of June. So… three months ago, give or take."

"*Roman*," Cole repeated, raising very judgmental eyebrows. But he sounded somehow satisfied, as though

Leo had confirmed something for him, potentially about how guys named Roman weren't to be trusted, judging by his next words. "Of course he's a Roman. No self-respecting obscure would have a name like Paul or Richard. *Roman.*" He shook his head. "It's like they want people to know." He sighed. "Roman. All right. And Roman was…?"

"Vampire."

"A vampire." Cole flipped open the pizza box. "Pineapple!" he exclaimed. "Brave choice."

Leo fought the urge to fidget. "I thought, you know, the candy store…."

"Good guess!" he said cheerfully, pulling a pair of plates from the cupboard. "Nature's candy, right? Excellent on pizza. Perfect complement to the salt." He paused. "You're not one of those heathens who eats pizza with a fork, are you?"

"Not unless I'm eating it while wearing a suit." Leo liked casual eating, but he liked his suits more.

Cole passed him a plate. "Sensible. You want a beer?"

And not have to be dead sober when he explained his predicament? "Please."

They sat at the kitchen table, Leo with his beer and Cole with a glass of milk. "Hate to let you drink alone, but I've had a rule against mixing magic with alcohol ever since Mom accidentally turned a garter into a scorpion at Cousin Julie's wedding."

Leo paused with a mouthful of pizza, then slowly resumed chewing. "Is that something you have to worry about?" he asked after he'd swallowed. He couldn't imagine that. Never being able to cut loose and just relax, always needing to be on guard.

"Nah. Mine's not an active power. The worst thing I'd probably do is disenchant somebody's makeup glamor. But it pays to be cautious."

Leo took a healthy swig of liquid courage. He hoped it wasn't rude to ask, but Cole seemed fairly open. "So how does it work, exactly? You say you don't have an active power, but your mom's is. Are there people who can do both? Like more than one thing?"

Cole waggled his head, tearing a paper towel from the dispenser in the middle of the table. "It sort of depends. You know how there are some people who are just good at everything? Good-looking, captain of the football team, 4.0 GPA, and somehow you still don't hate their guts?"

Leo had frozen guiltily with his slice of pizza halfway to his lips and his mouth open. Cole might as well have been reading from his high school yearbook.

Cole groaned. "Okay, presumably you're familiar with one of those individuals. Magic is kind of like that. Some people are kind of good at a lot of things. Some people can only do one thing really well. Sometimes they can only do one thing and are still kind of crap at it."

"So which category do you fall into?" Leo tried to guess. "I mean, there's the cursebreaking thing and… whatever you did with the lights, right?"

"What I did with the lights?" Cole repeated. Milk lined his upper lip in a ridiculous mustache, which he mostly wiped away with paper towel. Then he grinned. "You mean the motion sensors?"

Oh. Leo maybe should have thought of that. His ears burned. "So much for that 4.0 meaning anything."

"Eh, don't feel bad. Brave new world and all that. No, I have a couple other abilities, but nothing major. When I was a kid, my family thought I was a muggle."

Leo stared. "Wait, muggle, that's an actual term you use?"

"Nah, but when Harry Potter got big, we started to use it. Raises fewer eyebrows and everyone knows what it means. Mundane's the proper word, but it's, well…."

"Mundane?"

"Exactly."

"So your family thought you didn't have magic?" Leo prompted. This seemed like a story he wanted to hear.

"Let's just say they decided it was a good idea for me to learn a muggle trade, just in case."

And he picked making candy. Not exactly the most lucrative endeavor, but it was sweet.

Cole wiped a bit of sauce in the corner of his mouth with his thumb. "What about you?"

Leo blinked. "I've always been a muggle." He thought he'd been clear on that point.

"No, I mean, do you work?" Cole made a face. "Is that gauche? I don't do a lot of small talk outside of sugar-adjacent subjects."

Oh, right. "I work at the hospital. Nurse. I got off shift an hour before I went to see you at the store." The twelve-hour days had been a bear to begin with, but he was used to it now and couldn't imagine working the kind of job he had to do five days a week instead of three or four.

On reflection, no wonder he'd thought pineapple on pizza was an acceptable risk. His blood was probably 60 percent coffee right now. And that beer was going to hit hard too. It had been a long week.

"You're not going to pass out on me, are you?" Cole asked as Leo set his beer farther away from himself. He didn't need the temptation.

"Not on purpose. But I've worked just under fifty hours in the past four days." And now that he didn't have the adrenaline rush of worrying someone was going to think he was a lunatic for believing magic was real, he was going to crash.

Cole set down his pizza crust and dusted flour off his hands. "Gotcha. Well, let's get to it, then."

All at once, Leo's apprehension came rushing back. "Just like that?"

Cole shook his head and stood, a self-deprecating smirk twisting his features. "Come on. I'll show you where the real magic happens."

Chapter Three

"IT'S not the fancy kind of setup my gran has." Cole pressed his hand against the door to the altar room. "But then again, my needs are pretty simple."

At his touch, the door unlocked and swung open. Beside him, Leo froze. "Uh, so that was magic."

Cole cocked his head. "You used to let a guy drink your blood, but me opening a door freaks you out?"

"I'm not freaked out!" Leo protested. He wavered a little on his feet.

Yeah, Cole was glad he'd told Niamh to roost outside tonight. He waved Leo forward. "Come in and sit down. This could take a while."

Cole hadn't been kidding: his setup was pretty minimal. Gran's altar room featured velvet curtains, gas wall sconces, and a pentagram inlaid in colorful wood. Cole had vinyl blinds, LED candles, and a rug Kate had woven into a pentagram pattern for him, because before he'd bought the house, he'd lived in an apartment where he couldn't make any permanent alterations and his landlady liked to stop by and chat. He didn't bother with the candles now, though, just gestured Leo to the armchair he'd set in the center of the rug.

Leo hesitated at the edge of the circle.

Oh boy. Cole didn't often work with mundanes so unfamiliar with his world that he had to tell them everything. "It's a protection symbol," he said. "And in this case it will help magnify my ability to see the spell you're under. I can't do anything to you while you're standing inside it. Not unless I'm in there with you."

Leo had entered the pentagram and was lowering himself into the chair when a voice said, "What the hell, Cole, it smells like patchouli in here," and Leo almost hit the ceiling.

Damn it.

"I told you to stay outside!" Cole hissed.

Niamh alit on his shoulder, ruffling her feathers. "I never get to meet your company," she sniffed, beak clacking. "It's like you're ashamed of me." She drew out the *sh*; the shape of her mouth meant it came out almost as a whistle.

"Or it's like you're a talking bird and that's kind of a lot to dump on a guy who just learned about the obscure world three months ago."

Leo sat the rest of the way down.

"You *just* pointed out that he let a guy drink his blood." Niamh ruffled again before settling. "I thought he could handle it!"

"I'm still here," Leo protested. His tone reminded Cole of a wet kitten.

"Niamh."

"*Fine.*" She took off toward the open kitchen window.

Cole let out a long breath. "I'm gonna put in a screen," he muttered under his breath. "Freaking magpies." Then he recentered and closed the door behind him. "Sorry for the interruption. Familiars are notorious busybodies."

"Familiars," Leo said. "Animals that talk. To witches."

Cole should have fed him more alcohol. Or offered one of Gran's special candies. "Do you want to do this another time?"

Leo exhaled and visibly reined himself in. "No. I'm okay. It's just been a long week." He shook his head. "What do you need me to do?"

With his foot, Cole reached out and snagged the rolling stool next to the door. He pulled it toward himself and sat, then hit the dimmer switch. He didn't *really* need the candles, but low light would let him see the spell better. "Just sit, for now. The pentagram acts sort of like the UV light in those crime shows, you know?"

Leo made a face and squinted down at his chest. "Uh...."

"Never mind." Cole sat and closed his eyes, centering himself. Under the pentagram's magnification, the spell buzzed unpleasantly, setting his teeth on edge. "So. Tell me about you and Roman."

He heard Leo shift in the armchair. "Not much to tell. We met at a bar."

Oh, so it was like that. Cole hummed in acknowledgment and listened to the changing pitch of the spell. "Which bar?"

"No. I don't think so, at least."

Cole rephrased. "The name of the bar was?"

"Oh! Nightshade."

Cole couldn't help it—he opened his eyes. "The bar's called Nightshade and you don't think it's a—whoa."

The curse glowed a lurid green, casting an eerie halo around the armchair. Two bands wrapped around Leo's mouth almost like a gag and then, judging by the angles, crisscrossed behind his neck. They bound his arms, his chest, his hands, his legs. His dick. And they kept crossing, back up, until they met again over the left side of his chest.

That was *some* spellwork.

"What?" Leo asked, looking down. "Is it that bad?"

Cole shook his head. "I reiterate: you really pissed someone off." Someone who knew what they were doing with their craft too. But that would wait until later. "So you met Roman at a bar. And?"

"And what?" Leo challenged, his cheeks pink. Unfairly, the flush only made him more attractive. "I'm the victim here!"

"I'm not trying to slut-shame you or anything," Cole said quickly, hoping that was the problem. "But the more I know about your relationship, the better I'll be able to figure out the spell." He already had an idea of *what* it did. But the why would be instrumental in figuring out how to undo it.

"Oh." Leo deflated. "Sorry, I'm really…. It's been a brutal few months, and I feel stupid about it."

Cole had experienced his own share of romantic trauma—he could definitely relate. "Tell you what. How about we trade horror stories? Then it's not such a one-sided thing. I've got some doozies dating back to my childhood. Deal?"

Leo smiled, cheeks dimpling, and for a moment, under the magnification of the pentagram, he glowed pink instead of green, and the knot of spellwork twitched. "I think I'm getting the better end of this deal, actually. All right. I met Roman at Nightshade in June, and I invited him home with me."

Without intending to, Cole made a noise in the back of his throat.

"Yeah, rookie mistake, right?" Leo shook his head. "In my defense, I didn't know vampires were a thing. Not until he was an inch deep in my femoral artery, anyway."

Cole didn't mean to pry, but he was *looking* at Leo, and Leo was sitting in a pentagram, and it was impossible not to see the way his whole aura pulsed a heated red at the memory. Warmth rose in the back of Cole's neck, and he ran a hand over his hair, grateful for the low light. He was probably so blotchy right now. Jeez. "That's not very polite."

"No, it's not, though I wasn't complaining at the time," Leo admitted sheepishly. "We had words afterward, though."

"I can imagine." Fortunately Cole had never had to explain magic to a boyfriend or even a one-night stand. Unfortunately that was because he always got his heart broken before things got that far. "My turn. Let's see. My freshman year of high school, we were supposed to collect specimens for a project. My lab partner was"— *like you*—"popular, handsome, junior varsity basketball team. We were identifying our finds at Gran's and I was trying to get the nerve to ask him out to lunch, when suddenly the dead frog in front of him kicks and hits his hand. He screamed like a banshee and ran out of the house. I had to finish the project myself."

Leo's eyes were wide, even as he seemed to be fighting off giggles. "Your grandmother brought a frog back to life to fuck with your love life?"

"She didn't bring it back. She's not that evil. She just made its legs twitch a little." Cole shrugged ruefully. "He kind of deserved it. I'm pretty sure she overheard him ask me if she really was a witch like everyone said."

Leo grinned. "So you never asked him out?"

Cole shook his head. "I was gonna try it anyway, but he'd never meet my eyes after that. Either he thought *I* was the witch or he was super embarrassed about hitting a pitch that could shatter glass."

"Or he decided to respect the magical cockblock."

"Or that."

"My turn again." Leo leaned his head back against the chair. "Where was I?"

"Having your femoral artery perforated."

"And the ensuing 'vampires are real' conversation, yeah. In retrospect, I probably should've called the cops. Random pickup turns out to be a creature of the night? But on the other hand, what are they going to do? Do they carry garlic spray? Would that even work?"

Cole couldn't believe Leo was still alive. "You didn't kick him out."

Leo fidgeted. The edges of the halo went orange. "I asked him out for coffee."

A beat. Two. Cole took his time schooling his face and voice. He didn't need to put Leo on the defensive again. Finally Cole said, "Why?"

Leo flushed. "The sex was good! He seemed nice! I don't know, you don't go around telling just anyone you're a vampire, right? I thought we had a connection."

With some effort, Cole closed his mouth without saying anything. Deep breath in. Long breath out. Crap, he needed another embarrassing story. "When I was sixteen, I begged to borrow Gran's car for a night so I could take my friend Jamie to the movies."

Leo let that hang for a moment before he prompted, "And?"

"And she accidentally left a limburger sandwich under the passenger seat. It was August."

"No movie magic that night, huh?"

"No movie magic that *summer*," Cole lamented. Not until the summer after he turned seventeen, when he defied Gran's wishes and took a job as a counselor at a sleepaway camp. Mom had said Gran couldn't shelter him forever, and he was going to have to learn to get by in the mundane world on his own sooner or later.

Of course, Cole unwittingly removed a curse from his might-have-been-boyfriend co-counselor, and suddenly *everyone* found him super attractive and he didn't need Cole anymore.

Cole wasn't bitter.

Much.

Though after that, he knew he wasn't the genetic throwback of the family after all. "So. Coffee date?"

"Do you know how much daylight there is in June? Caffeine wasn't viable. Not if I didn't want to mess with my sleep schedule before work. But we went to a movie, caught a late dinner"—Cole refrained from asking whether Leo had *been* dinner—"and one thing led to another, and then it was July, and…."

"And suddenly you're dating a vampire?"

"I didn't see anything wrong with it. I'm an adult, he's…." Leo's mouth twisted and curled up in a wry admission. "Well, he's definitely old enough to make his own decisions. And it's nice being in a relationship. Having someone to come home to."

Oh holy Diana, he did *not*. "You moved in with him?" Not that most vampires weren't perfectly decent, but it didn't seem like Leo had made much effort to discern whether Roman was.

"No! I gave him a key."

Cole needed a minute to digest. How was Leo the guy who freaked out at talking magpies but also the guy who casually struck up a relationship with a vampire? The kind of relationship where he'd give someone a key within a month of meeting him? Cole was getting a headache just thinking about it.

He opened his mouth to counter with the time his prom date had an allergic reaction to Cole's boutonniere and started sneezing anytime he got too close, but what came out was "Seriously?"

Leo frowned. "I thought you weren't going to be judgy!"

"That was before I knew you gave a vampire a key after like one date!"

"I would've done the same if he were human!"

But he isn't, Cole wanted to say and didn't because, well. He didn't know Roman, and vampires weren't generally morally worse than the average mundane. "It's a miracle you've never been robbed," he muttered instead.

Leo went orange again. Cole decided not to ask for clarification and poked at Leo's thing with Roman a little further instead. "So what went wrong, anyway? Why'd you break up?"

Apparently Leo had forgotten this was supposed to be tit-for-tat. He shrugged. "The same thing that always goes wrong, I guess? We weren't working out. I didn't love him and vice versa. So we broke up."

That sounded fake, but that could just be Cole's personal biases coming into play. "No hard feelings?"

"Why would there be? Nobody cheated, nobody lied, nobody was an asshole. At least not until afterward, when I ended up with this... thing."

And Cole would get to the effects of that in a minute. But first, one more question: "So when was the last time you saw Roman?"

"Must've been about two weeks after we broke up," he said, obviously thinking back. "Yeah. He came by my place to grab a shirt he left there."

"And what were you doing at the time?"

Leo frowned. "Cooking, I think? I was working the day shift and Miguel came by for dinner."

Bingo. That smacked of motive. "Miguel?" Cole asked neutrally, following the threads of the curse as Leo spoke. Energy flowed along them, offering little hints.

"Yeah. The guy I dated after Roman."

The energy pulses all seemed to be heading in the same direction, culminating in a spiral around Leo's mouth. Cole's life would be a lot easier if humans would just pick up a book and learn about human— vampire, whatever—nature once in a while. "Well. The good news is I know why you got cursed."

Leo sat up straight. "That's awesome." And then he sagged again, slouching even more than he had previously. "What's the bad news?"

Cole stood and stretched the kinks out of his back. He needed to get a more comfortable chair. "You broke the cardinal rule of interacting with vampires: you hurt his pride."

Chapter Four

COLE let Leo out of the creepy pentagram chair, and they moved to the cozy living room. Leo kept looking for evidence of witchiness—sage bunches by the fireplace or upside-down crosses or more pentagrams or what-have-you—but no. Just a cozy overstuffed sofa, a worn armchair with a hand-knitted throw over the back, and... okay, the bird perch in the corner was a little witchy.

"So the curse," Cole said conversationally. "What's it do? Be as specific as you can."

Leo looked at him incredulously. "I was in that chair for half an hour. What were you *doing*?"

"Looking at it objectively. Now tell me what it does. I'm curious."

He had to have some idea, at least Leo hoped so. He sighed. "It—sort of makes me tongue-tied? I don't mean that I don't know what to say. I know what I want to say, but I can't get the words out."

"All the time, or in certain situations?"

Right, he had to be specific. "Like if I see a hot guy at a bar and I want to buy him a drink. I can't. Or ask for a number."

Cole nodded. "Anything else?"

Oh yeah. Lots. Leo counted off on his fingers. "Can't give anyone my number—not that anyone has even asked, though a few guys have looked like they're interested." If no one was asking for Leo's number, that was *definitely* part of the curse. "Can't even go dance with a guy I want to get to know. If I *do* start dancing by myself and someone comes up to me, I move away. I can't stop it. And I can't even count the times a guy has come up to me and said 'Can I get your' or 'Do you want' and not been able to finish the sentence."

"So essentially, you're magically cockblocked."

Leo let his head drop back against the sofa. "Pretty much."

Silence reigned for a few heartbeats. "So can you jerk off?" Cole finally asked, and Leo gave himself whiplash turning his head so hard. His ears felt like they were on fire.

"*What?*"

"I'm just, you know." Cole's light brown cheeks had gone a blotchy red, and he was staring at the wall over Leo's shoulder. "How urgent is this? A guy can go without getting laid pretty much indefinitely, but if you can't even relieve the pressure yourself, that could be, uh, unpleasant. So how urgently do you need this curse broken?"

Fine. Leo supposed that was a fair question. It still chafed him to admit, "Not *that* urgently."

"Okay. Well. Good. I'm happy for you."

Leo wondered if he could ask for another beer. Then again, he was already crashing. He just wanted to go home, crawl into bed, and pass out for twelve or thirteen hours. "So. How do I break it?"

Cole rubbed his temple, looking away. "It's not that easy. I have a couple of leads, but I want to run them by a friend of mine for feedback before I get your hopes up. I don't want to tell you it's simple and then it turns out you have to strip naked, bathe yourself in lamb's blood, and dance under the light of the new moon wearing a necklace of your own baby teeth."

Leo blanched. "Is that a possibility?"

"In your case it's just an example, but it wouldn't be the weirdest way I've ever broken a curse."

Leo decided not to ask. Not now, at least. He wanted to be able to sleep tonight. Maybe in a week, when he had a little distance and perspective.

"Well, that might be enough to turn me into a vegetarian, but if it breaks the curse…."

Cole grinned. "Don't worry. If it's going to come to that, I'll let you know and we'll get it out of the way before the frost. Bit self-defeating otherwise."

Oh God.

"Right." Leo shook his head. He was falling asleep, and he didn't think his dreams would be restful. "I should go before I pass out. Today has been… well, I was on my feet keeping patients alive and comfortable for twelve hours of it, and you were there for the rest."

Cole stood. "I'll see you out."

Leo barely remembered the drive home. He kicked his shoes off inside his apartment door, left his jeans in a puddle in the living room, and face-planted on the couch. He was asleep before his eyes had closed.

COLE closed the door to the yarn shop behind him and did a quick scan. Nobody but Kate, sitting behind a giant walnut desk piled high with yarn, needles clacking away at something in bright orange.

She raised her eyebrows over horn-rimmed glasses.

Cole locked the door, crossed the shop, and dropped into the chair on the opposite side of the desk. Then he laid his head against the smooth walnut and thumped it a few times.

"You should've gone into theater," Kate told him, clacking on to the next row of whatever it was.

"Shut up," Cole muttered into the desktop.

For a few seconds the only sound was the rhythmic tap of knitting needles. Cole let that soothe him, breathed in the years of magic that had soaked into the desk and walls, the scents of sage and lavender wafting in from the back room. Kate let him be until the tension had bled from his shoulders and he lifted his head to say, "True love's first kiss."

Not much fazed Kate. She hadn't batted an eye when Cole came out, or when it turned out he was a bit magic after all, or when he broke a family curse that had been active for generations. Now, though, she stopped knitting and put down—maybe a hat? Cole had never gotten the hang of knitting. He always managed to be surprised whenever she finished.

"What?"

"Right?" Cole said, sitting up now and waving his hand expansively. He knocked over a basket of magenta angora, which toppled to the floor with a series of very soft thumps. "I mean. I've broken a lot of curses, but I have never actually seen the cliché, you know? This is just… overcommitment to detail."

Kate inclined her head and the basket returned to its place on the corner of the desk, the yarn stacking itself neatly inside. Show-off. "This is the guy you want to…."

Cole started to wave his hand again to encompass the many varied things he would like to do to Leo, but he caught himself before he could make another mess. "Yeah, him. Kate, you should see this curse." She couldn't, of course; cursebreaking wasn't her gift. Cole would have to draw it for her. "There's no way anyone managed this without a focus object, maybe more than one. Are you sure no one's bought anything suspicious?"

Slowly, she shook her head. "You're thinking what? Lily petals? Basil? Camphor?"

Cole didn't think so. "It's stronger than that. Robust. Chestnut, maybe, with jute for flexibility?" He wrinkled his nose. He wasn't any better at crafting spells than Kate was at breaking them. "Not ringing any bells?"

"No, but that only rules out someone buying them here. There's always Amazon. Or petty theft."

"Or the hardware store," Cole pointed out. Jute wasn't exactly hard to come by. He sighed and laid his head on the desk again.

Kate picked up her knitting and resumed clacking. "So," she said cheerfully, "you gonna break it?"

"Am I going to—" Cole sat up. "Am I going to, what, casually make this guy fall in love with me and then kiss him?" Either she'd lost her mind, or she had a vastly inflated opinion of him. Cole's romantic history spoke for itself.

"You've had worse ideas," she said reasonably. "Remember that time you made peanut-butter mints?"

"First of all, I was twelve. Second, you haven't seen this guy, okay? He is not interested in this." He gestured to himself, this time without upsetting any textiles. "And anyway I don't date anymore."

Kate opened her mouth, probably about to start the usual argument—Cole didn't need clairvoyance to know that—but he interrupted with his final point.

"Besides, that would be unprofessional, right? There's more than one way to break a curse. If I can't untie the knot, I'll cut the threads. Or wiggle them until they're loose enough to pull off."

Clack, clack, clack went the knitting needles. "Kissing sounds easier." She lifted her gaze to his for a moment and quirked a smile. "And more fun."

"You do it, then," Cole grumbled, but he conceded the point. He needed to open the shop anyway. He stood and brushed yarn fibers from the front of his shirt. "Thanks for listening to me vent."

Kate nodded, clacking away. Then she slowed, rested the unfinished project on the desk, and met his gaze.

"You'll let me know if anything suspicious…?" Cole trailed off.

Kate's gaze darted to the door to the back room. "Course," she said. "Can't have people just running around magically… what? Putting people in chastity belts?"

Cole's life was so weird sometimes. He laughed nervously. "Yeah. Well. I better go open the shop now."

Kate nodded again, and the door unlocked. "You coming to Sunday dinner?"

The last time Cole had skipped, he'd intended to plan a romantic surprise for his boyfriend; instead they'd had a huge fight about bedsheets and broken up. "I'll be there."

THE problem with being chronically unable to hook up was that it put a huge crimp in Leo's social life.

At first he didn't mind it. He didn't pick someone up every night when he was single, and dancing helped release the tension that built up over a long workweek. But eventually having to go home alone got old. Eventually he started to grit his teeth when his friends left him at the bar by himself and went home with their evening's company. And eventually his friends got tired of him being tired.

Leo needed new friends, obviously. And some caffeine.

Too bad the guy across from him at the café—an attractive man whose too-short haircut made his ears seem very prominent—couldn't take a hint.

"Is this seat taken?" he asked with what he probably thought was a winsome smile but seemed pretty smarmy to Leo.

He barely even needed the curse's prompt to lie. "Sorry, I'm waiting for someone."

Between the curse and Leo's dour demeanor, that usually worked. Apparently today was his lucky day. "I'll keep you company while you wait." He pulled out the chair and sat on it backward, facing Leo. Had Leo found this behavior charming once upon a time? Had he done this to other people? Maybe he deserved this curse. "I'm Alex."

Leo debated telling Alex to get fucked, but the curse might misinterpret that as an invitation and leave him gaping like a fish. "Hi." He raised his mug to his lips, intent on ingesting his coffee before it got colder.

"Aren't you going to tell me your name?"

Leo was going to tell him something, all right. "I'm—"

"Sorry, sorry," a familiar-looking woman said, setting a porcelain mug on the tabletop. Leo couldn't quite place her. "The barista accidentally used the fat-free whipped cream and had to make me a new one." Leo had been watching idly; she'd done no such thing. "I'm Amy. And you are?" She said this sweetly, but the knife edge lurked just under the words, providing plenty of bite.

Alex scowled. "Leaving, apparently." He stood, the chair scraping unpleasantly against the floor.

Leo and Amy both watched him go. Then Amy shook her head and looked at Leo. "Charming character. Love the ears."

"Wish he'd used them to fly away," Leo joked, then immediately felt a bit mean. "Thanks for the assist. Cafés are as good as dance clubs these days, apparently." He corrected himself. "Or as bad."

"You looked like maybe an intervention wouldn't come amiss, and I need the karma anyway. I have fifteen minutes until my next clients, and they're…."

"Particular?" Leo suggested, offering his preferred euphemism for difficult patients.

"To put it kindly." She shook her head. "Locally made candy for the favors isn't going to cut it. They're going to ask for organic licorice or artisanal free-range chocolate or something."

Now Leo remembered where he'd seen her before—in Cole's shop the other day. "Artisanal free-range chocolate does sound delicious." Then he realized she was still standing beside his table as the café filled up. "Do you want to sit with me for a few? I promise I won't use a single cheesy pickup line." Easiest promise he'd ever kept—even if he were interested in women, the curse would hold his tongue.

"You're sure I'm not interrupting? I know how important it is to commune with one's coffee."

Shaking his head, Leo pulled his cup toward himself to make room. "I could use some human company." Oops. He hadn't meant that to come out as speciesist. Did Amy know about the arcane world? He only meant— "I've just realized too many of my friends are like our recently departed Alex."

Amy sat. "Tough realization." She took a quiet sip.

Worse, Leo didn't know that he was any better. Introspection sucked. "I'll get over it." He couldn't tell her much about the situation without giving away the existence of magic, and he didn't want to monopolize the conversation anyway. "So your clients… tough customers?"

With a sigh, she shrugged. "It's not so bad really. They hired a wedding planner, but they are the ones doing all the planning, down to the minute detail. I just make phone calls."

"So it's boring."

"Yes! But I feel bad complaining about easy money." She shrugged again. "My life would be simpler if Cole would branch out into chocolate, but he refuses. Nut allergy."

"The nerve." Truth told, Leo preferred chocolate, but he wasn't about to tell Cole that. Definitely not before he broke the curse. "But weren't you just wishing for more challenging work?"

Amy set her cup down. "Touché. Maybe I should put an ad on the internet? 'Charming small town seeks hipster chocolatier'?"

Leo laughed. "Couldn't hurt."

By the time Amy left for her appointment, Leo had a new friend and a light heart. Vowing to forget about magic and vampires and curses for the rest of the afternoon, he put his mug on the return cart and stepped out into bright September sunshine.

Across the street, the florist was setting up a display of autumn wreaths. Leo waved and the florist waved back.

A monarch butterfly landed on the flowering bushes along the sidewalk. The next house down, a realtor was hammering a For Lease sign into the yard of a two-story building that had once been a doctor's office.

Everything was bright and sunny and warm and beautiful, and Leo had an invite to games night at Amy's, where she promised no one would try to hit on him. He had another two days off to relax before work sucked him back in. The breeze coming off the lake ruffled his hair and kept the heat from becoming oppressive. It should have been a perfect day.

So why couldn't he shake the feeling that he was being watched?

Chapter Five

"GRAN?" Cole poked his head out the back door of the enormous Victorian two-story he'd grown up in. As far as he could tell, Gran wasn't in the house—not unusual, given the weather and the fact that she was ungodly spry for ninety-two. "I brought your gumdrops."

From the bench by the koi pond under the willow, she waved at him. Cole left the box on the kitchen counter, careful not to disturb the bundle of chicory she'd set out, and joined her.

"You're later than usual," she observed, her countenance neutral, but Cole detected the sharpness underneath. Gran might be nearing a hundred, but nothing got past her.

"I have a case," Cole said smoothly. He'd learned long ago that the only way to lie to his grandmother was to tell the truth. He *did* have a case. It simply hadn't made him late today. Well, unless you counted the extra time he'd taken to make the gumdrops because he'd fallen into an idle daydream about Leo.

Gran had spent over a decade thinking Cole was going to take after his mundane human father; Cole using his magic was a weakness of hers. "You're a good boy," she said. "Anyone I know?"

Cole caught himself before he could answer and looked into the pond. Three fat white-and-orange fish lazed in the water. The black-and-orange one twitched its tail and gobbled down a bug that had settled on the surface. "I don't think so." Any detail he offered would give away his attraction. He didn't want to dwell on his love life or lack thereof, and if Gran suspected, by God, there would be dwelling.

"Well." She pushed herself up before Cole could offer to help. "Since you're here, you'll stay for supper."

Cole stayed for supper every Friday. "Yes, Gran."

"I'm going to get started in the kitchen. Would you mind cutting a bunch of those cornflowers for me? I need to start putting them up now, or I'll run out of drying room."

Cole didn't roll his eyes. She asked him to harvest something every week. "Yes, Gran."

"The boline is on the porch!"

Probably right where he'd put it after he'd sharpened it last week. Shaking his head, Cole stood to get the knife.

Gran had a proper witch's garden. It rambled, and weeds grew unimpeded because when the herbs fought for resources it made their magic more potent. Cole set the gardener's mat on the grass next to the cornflowers—just going to seed now, as summer came to a close—and grasped a handful of flowers close to the ground.

The boline wasn't strictly necessary. Cole used regular garden shears on his own herbs, and they were just as effective. But Gran liked her traditions, and Cole had been harvesting her crop since he was a boy. He cut the flowers seven to a bundle and tied them with the twine wrapped around the boline's handle: five times around, one for each point on the pentagram.

Cole set down the seventh bundle and wiped his hands on his jeans, debating. The laurel next to the house swayed gently in the breeze, filling the air with its pungent scent.

Cole had grown up in that tree, climbing it, swinging from its branches. It shouldn't have been able to grow so far north, but *shouldn't* didn't count for much with Gran.

In the end, cowardice got the better of him.

"These gumdrops are just the trick for my arthritis," Gran praised when he came inside to hang the flowers. She bussed his cheek, then teased, "They might be even better than the original recipe."

Cole remembered having stomach cramps as a child and drinking Gran's foul blue cohosh tea. "You could've added some sugar," he teased back.

"Spoken like a man who has never dealt with children on a sugar rush."

That made him snort. "Did you forget what I do for a living? Children on a sugar rush are my bread and butter."

Gran laughed too, even though she'd spent the past few weeks trying to convince him that his calling was in alternative medicine. "That's my boy. Still terrorizing the parents of the neighborhood twenty years later."

"Hey, someone's gotta keep the dentist in cavities." He peered over her shoulder and sniffed appreciatively. "Need help?"

Gran swatted at him with a wooden spoon. "I may be old, but I'm not infirm. Go set the table."

Cole did what she told him. In the end, he always did.

WHEN the shop bell rang on Saturday, Cole was standing on a ladder behind the counter, filling a paper sack from one of the colorful jars. He eyeballed $1.25 worth of Swedish fish—or his version of them—then carefully climbed down to present them to his waiting customer.

"Thank you," the little girl whispered, clutching the bag to her chest with one hand and forking over a stack of quarters with the other.

"You're welcome," Cole told her, pretending he wasn't dying a little on the inside. She was *adorable*.

Her mother smiled at him and led the girl toward the door, and finally Cole allowed himself the luxury of looking over.

He didn't have the sight, not like Gran or even Kate. But he knew when he looked up he'd see—

"Hi," Leo said sheepishly, with a grin that lit his eyes.

Cole worked at not swooning. "Hi," he said back. "What brings you here? Sudden hankering for sweets?"

"Just coming back from brunch with Amy. Thought I'd check in and see if you'd made any progress?"

Cole had to work a little harder now to keep from betraying that he'd already worked it out. "I have a few ideas," he hedged. "I didn't know you and Amy knew each other." Amy had definitely played that pretty cool.

Leo shook his head. "New acquaintance. I'm broadening my horizons."

With the kind of life-altering events Leo had been through recently, Cole figured that made sense. "Club scene kinda sucks all of a sudden, eh?"

"You could say that. And all of a sudden I'm crazy jealous when my coworker gets a flower delivery from a secret admirer. Jimmy didn't even have a clue who it was from."

Cole had never been much of a fan of clubbing. He liked dancing, but the club scene made him feel self-conscious, which made it hard to let go and enjoy himself. "Well, I have good news and bad news, and then more good news."

Hooking a foot under the stool at the counter to pull it closer, Leo sat. "What's the good news? The first one."

"I know how to break the curse."

Leo brightened, or maybe the rest of the world just dimmed a little in comparison. "Seriously? What a relief." He laughed, and the tension that had held his shoulders just a shade too high relaxed and left him even more ridiculously handsome. Then he paused. "Why do I have a feeling about the bad news?"

With a wince, Cole admitted, "I know how to break it… but I can't actually *do* it." When Leo's face fell, he hurried to continue, "Which is fine! It's the kind of curse that will end in its own time. Meanwhile, I can try a few things to loosen it, and we might be able to get you out that way. And if you get to the end of your rope before then, I can break it by force—but I almost never recommend that."

Leo gave him the hairy eyeball. "Why not?"

Cole waved a hand. "Consequences. Scarring, illness, unpleasant pustules. One client got the hiccups for three days. Athlete's foot. A thunderstorm that knocked out power in three counties. Ooh, one time there was a microplague of aphids. Poor guy's garden has never been the same."

"Oh." Now Leo's shoulders were sagging. Damn. "Can you tell what the consequences will be?"

"Sometimes. Mostly not." Cole shrugged. "Some are worse than others, obviously. Sometimes nothing happens." In this case, he didn't want to find out firsthand if he didn't have to. Someone had put a lot of thought and effort into that spellwork. "I usually only recommend a force break if the curse is actively causing harm."

"Yeah. Well, I guess at the risk of athlete's foot, that makes sense," Leo joked weakly. "Did you say there was more good news?"

"I did! At least, there is if you like pie." He chose his words—and his mentality—carefully. He didn't want to fall prey to the curse.

Leo looked around as though he expected a pie to magically appear (which sadly Cole couldn't do), so apparently they were a go for pie. "I like pie."

"Good! And you're off work tomorrow?"

"Yeah, I go back Monday."

Perfect. "There's a festival two towns over—apple harvest. That means candy apples, apple donuts, apple turnovers… and more apple pie than you've seen in your life."

"Sounds incredible."

"And if you like hay rides, terrible carnival games, and second-rate handicrafts, it's even better."

Leo laughed. "Well, when you put it like that, it sounds like something I shouldn't miss."

"Pick you up at eleven?" Cole suggested. He tried not to sigh in relief when the words came out unimpeded. "The pie-eating contest is at noon, if you're interested in getting a stomachache."

"I think I'd rather leave the festival with my enjoyment of pie still intact," Leo said wryly. "But the rest sounds good."

Cole tried to say *it's a date*, his inner flirt winning out in spite of his best efforts, but the words didn't come. Of course. He shook his head to clear it. He should know better. "Great. See you then."

Chapter Six

SUNDAY morning promised what Leo considered unseasonable heat for mid-September, but maybe his delicate northern constitution just hadn't acclimated yet. He stepped onto his balcony in jeans and flannel, expecting comfort, only to immediately turn around and change into shorts and a T-shirt. He was just about to go downstairs to meet Cole when the glare of sun through the sliding doors suggested a ball cap might be an appropriate addition.

Cole arrived almost silently, in a tiny white car that made Leo do a double take until he realized it was electric. He let himself into the passenger seat, surprised to find his knees did not, in fact, hit him in the chin.

The fairgrounds were located, appropriately, in the midst of a huge apple orchard. Cole parked his pillbox between a battered Ford pickup and a soccer parent SUV, and they climbed out into the sunshine.

"So how come you've never been to the apple harvest before?"

"It's my first year here," Leo said. "I moved down from Toronto in January." Not, in retrospect, the best time to move house in Ontario; it had taken three hours just to get through London.

"No wonder you haven't had time to do more than clubbing." Cole locked the car and led the way toward a sea of booths. "This time of year there's something going on almost every weekend, but to be honest it's all agriculture related. Corn harvest festival, apple harvest festival. Oh, there's a monarch butterfly migration festival."

Leo looked over at him. "You're joking."

"No, they come through here in the tens of thousands. Look, we're not all fancy like Toronto; we have one club, two bars, a handful of gastropubs, and *this*." He waved his hand expansively, indicating—trees, mostly, and other green stuff, but Leo understood what he meant. "People need something to do."

"So they make pie."

"Hell yeah they make pie, city boy. Come on, we'll get you a sample. I hope you didn't eat an early lunch."

They passed a miniature tractor pulling a tiny train of plastic barrel cars full of children, and suddenly they were in the thick of things. A Johnny Cash cover band was playing on a stage at the far right; Leo felt for the lead singer, who'd donned a black suit for the occasion. Sweat prickled under his cap.

"So you've got your standard fair crafts," Cole narrated as they started down a row. "Kitschy home décor, some handmade pottery, some art. Last year I got this T-shirt."

Leo glanced at it—it was brown, a little lighter than Cole's eyes, and said *Hard Core*, with an eaten apple between the words. It was also a little snug; Leo could see the peaks of Cole's nipples. He looked away, the sun hot on the back of his neck. "Cute."

"You should see the apron."

Just as he said that, they passed a booth selling less *traditional* crafts, one of which was an apron with a lewd slogan. Leo cleared his throat.

Cole looked over. "Ugh, no, I wear it at work! Children might see it!" He said this loud enough that the stall owner looked up sharply and rolled her eyes. "Jeez," Cole said, this time at a lower volume. "Sorry I wanted someone to think of the children."

Leo snickered.

A few steps later Cole steered him into a tent where two older women were offering samples of various homemade jellies on crackers. Leo meant to save room for pie, but he accidentally stuffed his face with four different samples while Cole methodically read each label.

"These are amazing."

"This one's particularly good with pork," said the shorter of the two ladies. "It can be used as a marinade or a sauce."

Leo couldn't imagine using a jelly as either, but he decided it would make a nice snack with crackers and cream cheese when he came home from a late shift, so he bought a jar anyway.

"Sucker," Cole said. "That's going to sit in your cupboard for a year. Trust me, I know."

Leo didn't care. He was out. Having fun. With another person. "Didn't you promise me pie?"

"We're working up to it," Cole said loftily. "Want a pickle on a stick?" He looked like he wanted to say more, so Leo waited, but after a second Cole just let out an exasperated huff. "I don't even get to make a dirty joke? That's terrible, man. I'm sorry."

"We'll take it as understood," Leo said as they came upon the pickle booth. He didn't quite know what to expect until a tattooed man pulled a seven-inch skewered cucumber out of a barrel and presented it to a delighted kid. "But I'll pass anyway. Thanks."

Cole shrugged. "Suit yourself. One for me, please." He forked over five bucks and collected his prize.

"How are you going to have room for pie?"

"Don't be silly." Cole took an enormous, crunchy bite. Juice dripped down his chin, and an expression of utter contentment came over his features. He chewed slowly, then swallowed, obviously savoring every second, before wiping his chin. "I fasted."

No one ever died of blue balls. As a health professional, Leo knew this. But he still *felt* like he was dying inside. Cole wasn't even his normal type, though he was cute, with his broad, open face and brown eyes and naturally mussed hair. Then again, Leo's normal type turned out to be the kind of guy who cursed him for moving on, so maybe—

No. Once this curse broke, he was swearing off men for at least a month. And it wasn't fair to lust creepily after the guy who was volunteering to help him out in the first place and was going out of his way to make Leo feel like less of a loser. *Get it together.*

"Smart," Leo said finally, probably a beat too late.

Cole hummed happily, nodding. "Come on, I think I smell candy apples."

At the candy apple booth, Cole wanted Leo's opinion on four different glazes; fortunately the seller offered candied apple *slices*, so Leo could save both his fillings and his blood sugar. Sort of. "Too plain, wrong kind of apple," he said of the first, sitting at a picnic table safely out of earshot of the candymaker.

Cole hummed in acknowledgment as he chomped on his own slice.

Leo thought the second was pretty good, but Cole declared it too heavy on the cinnamon.

The third was salted caramel. Leo fell in love in a single bite. Cole must have seen it on his face, because he passed over his own slice.

Leo couldn't even muster the spine to politely decline. "Fank you," he murmured around the second and final bite, pulling Cole's slice toward him.

"Don't thank me," Cole laughed. "I'm getting a whole one." He didn't eat it right away, though, just asked for a wrapped one and put it in a bag.

They wandered through the rest of the fair, occasionally bumping shoulders. Leo ate too much pie. On the stage, not-Johnny-Cash gave way to a much more talented and less overdressed not-Linda-Ronstadt. Cole picked up a cork gun for his niece and a stuffed dog for his nephew, and Leo got in the spirit of things and purchased a few cheesy Christmas decorations.

"What?" he said defensively when Cole side-eyed his cheerful wooden reindeer. "It's cute, and I actually have room to decorate down here, unlike my place in Toronto."

"Whatever you say." His phone chirped, and he pulled it out of his pocket, his eyes going wide when he saw the hour. "Huh. Where did the time go?"

Leo was starting to regret that he hadn't put sunscreen on the back of his neck now that he'd been out in the sun for four hours. "Shit. I was going to do laundry before I go back to work tomorrow."

Cole turned in the direction they'd parked the car. "It's okay. I should probably take you home anyway. Gran is really intense about family dinners on Sunday."

Leo's parents had immigrated from Europe, but their families had stayed behind, so it was just them and his sister. "Yeah? Sounds nice."

"It is, until you skip a week and bad things mysteriously happen."

Okay, that *was* intense. "Your own grandmother cursed you?" Leo frowned.

"No, Gran would never." Cole made a thoughtful face. "Just, sometimes the universe likes things a certain way, and it makes it known when you're doing the wrong thing." He shook his head. "I guess that sort of thing doesn't happen to you? One time I tried to avoid breaking up with my boyfriend and ended up with strep throat. Couldn't kick it till I had a talk that was both literally and metaphorically painful."

Ouch. "Can't you just, you know, break that? Or brew some potion to make you all better or something?" Come to think of it, any number of his patients could probably benefit from some magical intervention.

Cole shook his head. "It doesn't work like that. It's tough to see your own curses, especially if it's just a tiny simple thing that'll wear off quickly. And magic can't cure a physical illness. It can only treat the symptoms." He glanced over as they passed the train cars again. "Sometimes I roll a potion into a batch of candy. Gumdrops for Gran's arthritis, mints for upset stomach."

"You should sell those at the hospital gift shop."

"Those aren't for sale. Probably have to market them as herbal remedies, what with the ingredients list. Allergies and all that. Can't be too careful."

Cole dropped Leo off and Leo retrieved his bounty from the miniscule trunk. They waved goodbye and Leo went upstairs to see about some crackers and jelly for dinner.

He was halfway through folding the first load of laundry when he realized he was still humming Linda Ronstadt.

AS always on a Sunday afternoon, Gran's was a paradigm of ordered chaos. Cole parked down the block, retrieved the pies from the back seat, and jogged into the family swarm.

"You're late," Kate hissed as he swept past her on the way to the dessert table set up on the porch.

"I have an excuse!" he half lied. He had been working, sort of, tugging at the bonds of the curse as Leo ate his way through candy apples and pie. He proffered the desserts. "And it's not like I showed up empty-handed!"

"That's a beautiful lattice top," Kate commented, taking the pie to set it next to Great-aunt Hilda's marshmallow salad. "Okay, I forgive you, but there's still Gran."

There was always Gran, but Cole didn't look for her right away. Instead he mingled, catching up with family. Julie was pregnant with baby number two and due to pop in November. Her first, Ella, hung on Cole's leg and gave him a running commentary: "Mommy's aura is green like plants 'cause she's gonna have a baby, but sometimes it's gray 'cause she didn't get enough sleep."

Cole scooped her up and sat her on his hip. "All right, little lady," he said, directing her to the rest of the family. "Give me the lowdown?"

Kate was dealing with a shipment mix-up—she'd ordered three boxes of merino and ended up with mohair.

"Orange," Ella whispered in that child's whisper that ensured everyone in a ten-foot radius could hear her.

Cole suppressed a smile. "What about me?"

Ella squinted at him, then squished his nose with one little finger. "Sunshine. With pinky streaks at the outsides."

How masculine. "Sounds pretty."

"You *are* pretty, Uncle Cole."

He play-bit at her fingers. "Thanks, pumpkin. Who should we do next, hmm? Your dad? Auntie June?" He lowered his voice. "What about—"

Behind him, someone cleared their throat. "You were late."

Damn. Cole spun around, Ella tucked into his shoulder, giggling. "I was getting pie," he said. "And working! Very serious business."

Gran harrumphed, but the hint of a smile lurked under the corners of her downturned mouth, and she couldn't hide it from Cole. "Don't be late again," she admonished, shaking her finger.

Ella's giggles tickled Cole's neck as Gran moved past to tend to the grill.

"What about *her*?" Cole whispered.

"Uh-uh." Ella shook her head.

Yeah, fair enough. Cole wouldn't risk crossing Gran either. "Good choice," he told her. "Let's go see what's cooking."

Kate found him later, over the day's second slice of apple pie, as Cole sat with Ella and her stepcousin Theo at the kids' table. "Gran says you were working this afternoon."

"This whole family is full of gossips," Cole said to Ella.

"As if you're innocent." Kate set her tarot deck on the table and looked at him expectantly.

Cole squirmed. "You wouldn't."

"Not if I don't have to," Kate agreed. Then she lowered her voice. "Gran's deck was out when I went into the dining room to grab a serving spoon earlier. Guess whose photo was on the table."

Damn. She never did like waiting to find things out in their own time. "You don't think I'm going to have to drop the case, do you?"

"No. But you might want to be careful about how much extra time you spend with your client unless you want to field questions about it."

Cole let out a long breath. "When I came over the other day I found her staring into the koi pond," he admitted.

Kate raised her eyebrows and twisted her lips in sympathy. "That thing's basically a widescreen TV when she uses it."

"Yeah." Of course Gran couldn't just use a crystal ball. She needed the bigger picture. Literally.

"So the question is." Kate tapped the deck. "You wanna know what she knows? Or what?"

Cole shook his head. "Not now. Not *here*." Not where Gran could overhear without even resorting to using magic to spy on him. And maybe he was better off not knowing, period. He and Kate weren't likely to get an exact duplicate reading anyway, and a little knowledge could be dangerous. "That could have consequences."

Shrugging, Kate picked up the deck and shuffled one-handed. "Fair." Then she tilted her head toward Ella, waiting for Cole to nod reluctantly before she said, "Maybe

Ella will save us?" She gestured over her shoulder, where Aunt June's husband, Todd, was taking advantage of his mostly captive audience to repeat the story of how an unexplained microstorm had made his colleague late for an interview, thus ensuring he got the promotion. Gran might be a bit scary, face-to-face, but she would never hold anything against a child.

Ella smiled at Kate and reached across the table, wordlessly flipping over the top card of the deck.

Justice, upside-down.

"You said it," Cole agreed. "I'm getting a beer."

Chapter Seven

BEFORE the curse, Leo hated working afternoons.

When he worked days, he had a more or less normal life. Get up, go to work, go home, go for a run, eat dinner, hang out with a boyfriend, rinse, repeat. When he worked nights, he slept late, then got up and ran errands, had dinner with his boyfriend, then went to work. Afternoons felt like this weird in-between place. It was late enough when he got home that if he did have a boyfriend, he was usually asleep when Leo arrived and gone before Leo got up. He couldn't go to dinner with friends. And he hated coming home in the dark.

After the curse, afternoons became a blessing. Leo had a handy excuse not to go dancing. He could tell himself—truthfully—that socializing didn't fit in his schedule. He wasn't being pathetic. No one cared if he just came home and went to bed, then watched Netflix in his boxers until it was time for work.

But for the past three days, Leo hadn't been able to shake the feeling that someone was watching him in the dark.

At first it was just the hair on the back of his neck prickling. He told himself it was nothing. His mind was playing tricks on him because suddenly the occult world had become part of *his* world.

Tuesday night there was a strange car in the parking lot when he got home. That might not have been unusual at a larger building, but Leo's apartment only had six units. And when he turned the light on in his apartment and glanced outside, the car's headlights came on and it drove away.

The next night he lay awake in bed for hours, exhausted and gritty-eyed, startling at every noise until finally he took a sleeping aid and closed the window.

With the chemical help, he slept soundly. When he woke Thursday the sky was clear and the air was crisp, and Leo put his paranoia out of his mind and went for a run.

Work went smoothly. He gossiped with his coworkers, prevented doctors from administering the wrong medication, taught a seven-year-old how to solve a Rubik's cube, and joined the nurses' fantasy hockey league, which would draft Friday. He even managed to sneak a few crackers with cream cheese and jelly from the fair for a snack. By the day's end he was as exhausted as usual, but he felt cheerful.

There were no suspicious cars in the parking lot when he arrived, wiping eyes bleary with want of sleep. He let himself into his building, made sure the door closed and locked behind him.

The stairwell echoed with his footsteps as he dragged himself up to the third floor.

And stopped.

There, on the floor outside his apartment, sat a bouquet of flowers in a beautiful glass vase.

"Okay, this is weird," Leo muttered. He couldn't go on dates or kiss guys or get laid, but people could send him flowers?

Maybe he shouldn't touch them. Maybe he should just turn around and go back to the hospital and sleep on a cot there. This whole thing would be ridiculous once the sun rose.

But he wanted *his* bed, dammit. His whole body ached for it.

Finally he huffed. There was no one in the hallway. So no one would think it was weird if he just—

He pulled off his scrub top and wrapped it around his left hand. Then, careful not to touch it with his bare skin, he picked up the vase. He unlocked his apartment with his other hand and set the flowers on the counter.

Moonlight spilled in through the balcony doors, limning the cozy space of Leo's open-concept apartment in just enough silvery detail for him to avoid bruising his shins. He set his keys down next to the flowers and kicked off his shoes.

The bright fluorescent kitchen light made him squint when he flicked it on, but he wanted to examine the flowers more closely. The kitchen drawer nearest the door held a first-aid kit, and he scavenged a pair of nitrile gloves. He'd have to ask Cole about spellproof materials, but for now....

There was a card, nestled between stems of bright yellow daffodils and ferns and tiny blue flowers. Leo teased it out, but it bore only the legend Peaseblossom, the flower shop across from the café.

Very, very weird, but not necessarily suspicious. It could just be a misdelivery. There was another apartment on his floor, after all. And wouldn't someone who was trying to hurt him remove the shop's card? Leo would check with the shop owner tomorrow and get the whole thing straightened out. In the meantime—

His stomach grumbled loudly, letting him know there'd be no peace until he'd eaten.

He pulled off the gloves and washed his hands thoroughly, just in case, before reaching for the half loaf of bread on the counter. He took out a slice and spread it with a thick layer of peanut butter, not bothering with a plate. Why dirty more dishes than he had to? There was no one here to judge him.

He was just swallowing the first creamy, chewy, peanutty bite when he heard it. A low rumble, faint but somehow pervasive. For a second the hair on the back of Leo's neck stood up.

But the next second it was gone. Leo paused with his slice halfway to his mouth, straining his ears for the sound.

He looked at the apartment door. He looked at the flowers.

Nothing. Just a trick of the night and his own overactive imagination, which had a little too much fuel lately. That was all.

He stuffed another bite of peanut butter bread in his mouth.

There it came again, this time louder. And longer. And *meaner*. It sounded less like a rumble now and more like a growl, animal and threatening and ominous.

Leo felt the hum of it in his teeth, in his bones. Hair rose all over his body.

The sound went on, almost a howl, the frequency of it making the flower vase rattle on the counter. It sounded *hungry*.

To hell with this, Leo thought. He grabbed his keys from the counter, shoved his shoes on, and booked it back to his car.

FRANTIC knocking interspersed with continuous doorbell ringing woke Cole from a dead sleep. He sat bolt upright in bed, heart pounding; then he looked at the clock. *The witching hour is upon us*, he thought grimly.

Niamh fluttered grumpily from her perch by the window. "Someone better be dead," she squawked.

"Bite your tongue," Cole grumbled, wiping a hand over his face. "Do you see my slippers?"

Still indignant, Niamh flapped to the open window.

"Don't you dare poop on whoever it is!" Cole shouted after her.

He'd best hurry down the stairs.

He found his slippers by tripping over them, but at least he wouldn't spend an hour trying to fall back asleep because his feet were cold. He took the stairs three at a time, spurred on by the pounding that would not stop. At the bottom of the stairs, the rug almost skidded out from under him, but he caught himself on the front doorknob. He allowed himself half a second to recover before he threw the door open.

Leo stood on his front step, shirtless, wearing only a pair of scrub pants and untied tennis shoes.

Cole gaped.

Who knew nurses had *that* much time to work out?

"Uh," he said. Apparently his brain was still upstairs sleeping.

The slap of wings on air snapped him out of his trance. "Invite him in, dumbass. It's freezing and he's basically naked."

Right. Cole stepped aside, gesturing Leo into the house. "Come in, come in, sorry. What the hell happened? Are you okay? What are you doing here?"

Niamh landed on Cole's shoulder as Leo stepped inside, and Cole closed the door and locked it.

Leo wrung his hands.

Oh boy. Cole hoped he had some lemon fizzies in the cupboard. Leo was going to need them. "Why don't you go and sit down and I'll get you something to wear." Not that any of Cole's shirts were going to fit, exactly, but they could at least keep him warm.

Leo went through to the living room, but he didn't seem like he was taking much in. When he sat on the couch, Cole muttered to Niamh, "Keep an eye on him, okay? I'll be right back."

"What do you think he's going to do? Faint?"

Cole seriously hoped not, but he made it up the stairs in record time anyway. He grabbed the first clean T-shirt from the shelf in his closet, then took the quilt off his bed for good measure. This would be an excellent time to have a few magic tricks up his sleeve, but he'd have to do this the mundane way, for the most part.

Leo hadn't moved by the time he got downstairs. Cole couldn't decide if that was a good sign. He handed over the T-shirt, which Leo put on as though on autopilot.

The shirt was powder blue and read Fruitier Than a Nutcake. It stretched so tight across Leo's shoulders Cole might never be able to wear it again—he swore he heard seams ripping. He could still count Leo's abdominal muscles.

Leo traced one of the pairs of cherries on the shirt. Then he looked up, seeming a little more composed. "Really?"

Cole shrugged. "I thought it was funny." He handed over the quilt, even though that felt like overkill now that Leo had color in his cheeks and clothes on his body. "You going to tell me what happened?"

Leo let out a long breath as Cole sank down next to him. Niamh took off from her spot on the back of the couch to her perch near the fireplace. "It's going to sound crazy."

"Probably not," Cole pointed out, trying to gauge whether he should have Niamh fetch the lemon fizzies. "Let's hear it."

With a shake of his head, Leo pulled the blanket around his shoulders. "At first I just figured I'd given myself the heebie-jeebies."

Heebie-jeebies? Cole bit his tongue.

"I could swear I felt someone watching me. That was Monday. Tuesday night there was a suspicious car in the parking lot when I got home."

Okay, that definitely sounded like heebie-jeebies. Maybe he'd just gotten a little too close to the paranormal world and it had freaked him out. Cole inclined his head toward Niamh.

She ruffled her feathers but made for the kitchen without complaint. Cole heard the scrape of talons on the counter as she picked up the cloth bag of sweets he kept for emergencies—though this particular emergency he had not foreseen.

To Leo, Cole prompted, "Go on."

Leo exhaled a long, slow breath, his cheeks puffing out. He was still shivering a little. "Tonight when I got home, there was a bouquet of flowers on my doorstep. There was a card from the flower shop, but no note. I don't know who could have put it there. You need a key to get into the building."

Cole caught the bag of sweets and murmured a soft thanks to Niamh, even as a chill went through him. Perhaps Leo hadn't overreacted. "Stand up."

Leo startled. "What?" He stood. "Why?"

"I want to make sure you didn't run into more trouble." But a quick scan showed just the same old curse. No new dangers. Cole shook his head. "You're clean. Well, apart from the one we already know about." He held out the bag. "Take a yellow one. It'll help with the nerves."

Leo did, sitting down again and pulling the blanket back around his shoulders. He still looked a little green, but at least the blue tinge was gone from his skin. "Thanks. Anyway, I thought the flowers were weird. But then I heard this... noise."

"What kind of noise?"

"Hah." Leo shook his head and popped the fizzy in his mouth. "I don't know. Some kind of animal. Never heard anything like it. Like a growl but almost... musical? It freaked me out." He closed his mouth around the candy and made a thoughtful face. "This is good."

"Thanks," Cole said, glad to have something he could comment on. Tonight was a full moon, but a musical growl? Did Leo have a cryptid singer-songwriter for a neighbor? "Anyway, stay here tonight. I don't have a spare room, but the couch folds out. It's comfortable."

Leo sighed and leaned back into the cushions. "I probably won't bother pulling it out. It's long enough if I curl up." He looked exhausted. And kind of... grimy.

"Did you go right home after work? No shower at the hospital?" Cole didn't know a nurse's usual routine.

Leo rubbed at his right eye. "Locker room shower's about like you'd expect." He quirked a rueful smile. "You'd think a bunch of nurses would be less gross, but no."

"I could draw you a—" *bath*, Cole wanted to say, but the word stuck in his throat. Apparently that was too sexy.

Leo looked like he was about to laugh, but he held it in.

Cole rolled his eyes. "Oh honestly. Do you want to take a shower? I have good water pressure and plenty of clean towels. I promise Niamh won't spy. Might help you warm up."

"If you're not offended, I think I'll just go to sleep." His eyelids drooped and he shook his head before narrowing his eyes accusingly. "What's in those candies?"

"Lemon and lavender, mostly." Magic made the relaxing effects of lavender much more potent. "How do you feel?"

He took a deep breath, his eyes closing all the way this time. "Tired," he sighed.

Cole patted him on the knee. "All right. Off to bed with you, then."

Niamh rode Cole's shoulder as he got up to go to the stairs. By the time he put his hand on the railing, he could see that Leo had kicked his feet up on the couch.

When the motion-sensor lights clicked off a minute later, they were both asleep.

Chapter Eight

LEO woke up staring into the beady black eyes of an American magpie. He wasn't sure who screeched louder, him or the bird. Either way, not an experience he wished to repeat.

Niamh flitted to the perch near the fireplace, having served her purpose. "Cole ran out to grab breakfast," she informed him, and wasn't that absurd? An animal was speaking to him. "He says there's a clean towel in the bathroom if you want that shower. I can show you where."

"Thanks." Leo sat up and stretched slowly, surprised to find himself refreshed. He hadn't woken the whole night, despite the troubles he'd had all week. Apparently his subconscious felt safe here.

Ugh, he couldn't believe he'd gone to sleep without his shower. "Bathroom's upstairs?" he guessed.

Niamh flapped over to the railing. "Follow me."

As Cole had said, she left him alone once she'd shown him the bathroom. Leo took advantage of some very nice toiletries—he was pretty sure the soap was handmade—and the promised excellent water pressure. The water stayed hot too. Maybe it was magic, he thought with a little laugh.

He was just drying off on a very thick, soft bath mat when he realized he didn't have any clean clothes.

Fortunately being a nurse had cured him of most of his body shyness. He wrapped the towel around his waist and opened the bathroom door.

And came face-to-face with Cole, who gave him a pained look. "Is accidental casual nudity going to be a thing with you?" But then he grinned to show he was teasing, or maybe he was just surprised he'd managed to get the line out around the curse. Maybe this was part of it loosening. "Follow me, I'm sure I can find something to keep you decent until we can raid your apartment for clothes that actually fit."

"You read my mind," Leo said wryly.

Cole waved that off. "Nah, not my trick."

Leo followed Cole into his bedroom, which was done in soft, soothing blues that felt mature rather than boyish. The bed was missing its quilt—which was probably downstairs on the couch, folded into a neat bundle, where Leo had left it. Cole, Leo noted, slept on the right side. Leo was a left-side sleeper himself.

He really needed to stop looking at the bed, and the barren left-side nightstand.

"Here." Cole opened a set of double doors into an enormous walk-in closet, which Leo thought was pretty hilarious, because he'd never seen Cole in anything but a T-shirt and jeans, give or take an apron. "Let's see…."

Cole bestowed Leo with a green T-shirt, this one featuring assorted vegetables and the slogan Lettuce Turnip the Beet, sweatpants that wouldn't reach Leo's ankles, Saturday day-of-the-week socks, and a pair of Andrew Christians. Leo could have done without knowing Cole went around wearing fancy underwear beneath his otherwise plain wardrobe. Or at least, he'd have preferred to find out under other circumstances. "Thanks," he managed.

Cole's mouth worked soundlessly for a moment before he said, "Oh for fuck's sake, I'll be downstairs when you're done."

This time Leo couldn't hold back the laughter.

When he'd dressed and went down to the kitchen, he found Cole swaying as he hummed tunelessly, setting out fruit and yogurt and bagels. "You hungry?"

Leo thought briefly of his aborted midnight snack, and his stomach rumbled.

"Thought so." Cole gestured to a couple of plates and bowls. "Help yourself."

Leo did, being extra generous with the yogurt particularly. "So what's the plan for this morning?"

Cole popped a bagel in the toaster. "Well, I have to open the shop, but I asked Danielle to come in early. Then I figured we'll check out your apartment, make sure it's safe. Investigate the source of your weird noise. After that, I guess we'll see."

Nodding, Leo spooned yogurt into his mouth. If he didn't say anything, he could trust his voice not to betray the anxiety he felt at the idea of returning to his apartment. Which was silly. What could happen to him in the light of day, with a trained cursebreaker at his side? Cole wasn't going to let anything happen to him.

Cole's bagel popped, and he hot-potatoed it onto a plate and reached for the peanut butter. "Bagel?"

Why not. He deserved six hundred calories of carbs after what he went through yesterday. "Please. Sounds great."

They met Danielle at the shop at quarter to nine, and Cole unlocked the door. At ten to, they pulled into the lot at Leo's building.

Leo fidgeted in Cole's diminutive passenger seat.

Cole turned the car off, but when Leo didn't move right away, he looked over. "You want me to go in first?"

Surprisingly, Leo did not. He unbuckled his seat belt. He didn't want Cole going in alone any more than he wanted to do it himself. "No, that's… I'll come in." He tried for a smile.

"That's the spirit." Cole got out of the car, and Leo found the courage to follow.

In daylight everything seemed perfectly innocent, even cheerful. The flowers outside the entrance were still in bloom. Leo unlocked the main door and let Cole precede him inside. "I'm on the third floor."

"No elevator?" Cole teased. "No wonder you're in such good shape."

Leo snorted. The stairs didn't do much, considering he walked up them maybe twice a day, but they did put Cole's behind at an excellent level for Leo's viewing. It provided a nice distraction until they reached Leo's floor and the horrible pit in his stomach opened again, threatening to swallow every iota of joy.

"Right or left?" Cole asked when Leo didn't move toward either door.

"Right." Leo reached into his pocket for his keys.

Cole held out his hand. Leo could have kissed him, except of course that he couldn't. "I'll get the door,"

Cole offered, and then he held out his other hand with the bag of candies.

"Thanks." Leo picked out another lemon fizzy, touched. Calm washed over him as the flavor burst on his tongue. He nodded at Cole to continue.

The door swung open.

Leo didn't know what he'd been expecting. Atmospheric ripped curtains or obviously rearranged furniture or some guy chopping a hole in the wall with an ax, then popping his head through to say, "Heeeeeeere's Johnny!"

He didn't get any of that. Just his apartment, exactly as he'd left it, as far as he could tell. Cole pocketed Leo's keys as though on autopilot. "Is it all right if I keep my shoes on? I don't want to take unnecessary risks."

"I'm not taking mine off. I don't want to touch things any more than I have to. You're fine."

"Great." Cole turned and looked at the vase sitting on the counter, but he didn't reach out to touch it. Instead he pulled two pairs of ordinary gardening gloves from his pocket and handed one to Leo. "Put these on, just in case."

Leo examined them as he did so. "Are they, like, lead-lined or something? Magic-proof?"

Cole smiled. "Sort of. They're cotton." He shrugged, then reached for the vase. "Neutralizes curses. Nature's protector, I guess. A T-shirt won't stop a curse someone's hurling at you any more than it would stop a knife or a bullet, but it protects from cursed objects like a T-shirt protects from a sunburn."

"Huh." Leo made a mental note to start keeping *these* in the drawer by the front door instead. "So? Anything?"

Cole lifted the flowers from the vase and held them over the sink to examine them. "Nothing on the flowers.

Actually, this is a strange collection. Daffodils—that's love, luck, and fertility." He glanced over, a wry smile on his features, but his cheeks were pink. "Someone who knows about your predicament, maybe? And the fern. Protection, health, blah blah blah. And forget-me-nots. True love and memories." He shook his head, then opened the cupboard over the sink and took down a glass, which he filled with water. He set the flowers inside. "I'd think you have a secret admirer, but I'm pretty sure a secret admirer wouldn't be able to send you these."

"So something weird, but not necessarily something dangerous." Leo fought the urge to fidget.

"Essentially." Cole turned back to look at the vase, frowning. "This, however…."

Leo took the opportunity to look at it in plain daylight. It was smallish, heavy-looking, maybe made of some kind of leaded glass. "Yeah?"

"This is definitely enchanted."

Despite the magic candy, Leo's stomach sank. But Cole was still holding up the vase, examining it in the sunlight, his brow creased. "I swear it looks…."

Leo wanted to prompt him, but Cole set it down again. "Never mind. Ready to continue?"

Continue? "Now what?"

Cole waggled his glove-clad fingers. "Looking for anything else suspicious. We're gonna toss your apartment. Don't worry, I'll let you do the bedroom."

For a second Leo weighed the pros and cons of searching for cursed objects by himself versus having Cole go through his sex toy drawer. Oh God, he really hoped none of *that* stuff was cursed. "But how will I know when I find something?"

"Well, it'll probably be something you haven't seen before. It's much easier to plant an object than to steal one, curse it, and put it back."

That would still mean someone had been inside Leo's apartment, but he accepted the explanation. "All right. And if I find something suspicious, I'll just...."

"Whistle?" Cole suggested. "Scream like a toddler? Calmly get my attention?" He shrugged. "Just don't touch whatever it is with your bare skin. Oh, and beware of dust bunnies," he added, pulling open a kitchen drawer seemingly at random.

Were dust bunnies a thing? "Why?"

"Hmm? Oh, no reason in particular. I just hate dust."

Well. All right, then. Armed with just enough knowledge to make him dangerous to dust bunnies, Leo entered his bedroom.

On first glance, nothing seemed out of place. Leo opened the curtains and looked behind them for anything that shouldn't be there but found nothing. The space under the bed contained no obvious cursed objects, though he did sneeze a few times, prompting Cole to call from the next room, "I warned you about the dust bunnies!" Leo pulled out a few lonely socks and was about to drop them in the laundry hamper when he realized he ought to dump that out too.

Clothes, more clothes, a towel, some spare change he must have had in a pocket. Nothing incriminating. Leo moved on to the nightstand drawers. Lube, condoms, passport—hmm, maybe he should put that somewhere else in case of spills—a couple of old photographs. The bottom drawer was empty; he hadn't brought much with him when he'd moved.

His closet was clean, aside from another colony of dust bunnies and some dirty clothes that needed to be rehomed. He tossed them in the hamper. And that was most of the bedroom taken care of. He poked his head back out to the living room to find the couch cushions on the floor and Cole on his knees in front of the couch, using his cell phone as a flashlight to peer into the crevices.

Perhaps Leo could be somewhat more thorough. He turned around again and pulled back the covers on the bed. Hell, he might as well put his sheets in the wash too while he was at it. He picked up a pillowcase and shook it to slide the pillow out. But when he reached over to grab the other one—the one he didn't sleep on—he felt something hard.

"Cole?" Carefully, Leo pulled the pillow and pillowcase apart. His mouth went dry, and his stomach twisted. What the hell…?

Cole appeared in the doorway. "What did you— oh." He peered over Leo's shoulder—a neat trick, seeing as he was several inches shorter—and then came around to his side. "Can I?"

Leo nodded, still holding the pillowcase open. Cole reached in.

The object was six or so inches long. At first Leo thought it was a cross. Then Cole turned it over and he saw the face.

His knees wobbled. "What is that?"

"You know what it is." Cole set it faceup on the bed. "It's you."

The tiny doll looked nothing like him. Oh, it had yellow hair—"Flax," Cole murmured—and blue eyes, and two legs and two arms. But the features were simply glued on a seed pod. "And winter cherry." He touched the doll's cheek. "Blackberry thorns. Boneset. Chicory."

"I need to sit down." None of that made any sense to him, but it made the hair on his nape stand up. Unfortunately it had the opposite effect on his spine.

Cole wrapped an arm around his shoulders and led him out of the bedroom. "Come on. You're gonna sit on the couch and I'm going to pack your bag."

"Am I going somewhere?"

"Well, you're not staying here." Cole picked up a couch cushion and put it back on the couch, then pushed Leo down on it. "Not if someone else can get in without you knowing, no matter their intentions."

Leo blinked at him, but Cole had already disappeared back into the bedroom. Leo could hear him opening drawers and pushing hangers around in the closet. "Intentions?"

"Flax. That's healing, protection. Blackberry too. Boneset, that's exorcism, drives away evil." Cole must have found Leo's overnight bag, because there came the sound of a long zipper opening. "And chicory. Removal of obstacles."

That sounded... not terrible. "Wait... what?"

"Different signature," Cole said. A drawer opened, closed.

"So... what does this mean?"

Another zipper sound, and then Cole appeared in the bedroom doorway, Leo's bag slung over his back. "No idea!" he said. "But whoever made it, it's not the person who cursed you, and it's not the person who sent that vase. Come on, let's get out of here."

Good idea. Leo got up, surprised to find that his knees carried him without any trouble.

They left the apartment, Cole with a bag of garbage to take down to the dumpster and an armful of flowers, Leo with his packed overnight bag. He hoped Cole had remembered his toothbrush and some scrubs. But if not, well, Leo could always go shopping.

On the second-floor landing, they ran into Leo's across-the-hall neighbor just coming in, sweaty from one of his dog walks. "Hey, Leo."

"Nate," Leo managed, thankful for programmed politeness. "How's it going?"

"Loving life!"

He always was. He was absurdly good-natured.

Leo and Cole continued to the ground floor and let themselves out of the building. Once Cole had tossed the garbage away, he squared his shoulders and said, "So about that noise you heard last night."

Oh great. "Yeah?"

"Probably nothing. Your neighbor needs some soundproofing. I can help."

Leo didn't ask. Cole popped open the trunk and Leo tossed his bag inside. "Now what?"

Cole untucked the flowers from the crook of his elbow. He'd wrapped the vase in Leo's scrub top from the night before for the trip down the stairs. He brandished the florist's business card. "Now we're going to find out what this guy knows."

Chapter Nine

PEASEBLOSSOM resided in a tiny building that had once been a carriage house but had been updated to include plumbing, shelving, and a lovely bay window that currently held a colorful display of Thanksgiving arrangements. Fortunately, at the moment, Leo and Cole were the only patrons.

The bell above the door rang cheerfully when they entered, which seemed a silly formality since no one in the place could have missed their entrance. Avery smiled at them from behind the counter—once upon a time that had made Cole's heart beat double time, but he'd spent enough time in Leo's company that he was becoming immune to extremely attractive men—and then something went *whap whap whap*, and Leo hit the floor as a knee-high gray blur ran out from the back of the shop.

"Hi," Cole said to Avery.

"Oh my God, hello, beautiful," Leo said to the dog.

Avery's smile widened, as though nothing in the world could possibly endear him so much as someone loving his dog. "Good morning, gentlemen. What can I do for you?"

Using the T-shirt, Cole set the vase with the flowers shoved haphazardly back inside on the counter, hoping Avery could see well enough to know he shouldn't touch it. "We're here to find out who sent these flowers."

Out of the corner of his eye, he noted that Tinkerbell had flopped over to beg for belly rubs. Leo didn't seem inclined to stand up. Maybe the combination of puppy magic and lemon fizzies was too much for his body to process.

Avery looked at the vase. Then he looked into the cooler on the wall to his left. Sure enough, it contained daffodils—unusually out of season—and forget-me-nots as well. But his eyes, so dark a blue they were nearly violet, held only confusion. "These were mine," he agreed, touching a finger to one of the blooms. He kept his hands well away from the vase. Then he gestured with his head to where Leo and Tinkerbell were getting better acquainted.

"Leo." Cole resisted the urge to poke him with the toe of his shoe.

Leo stood up, narrowly avoiding hitting his head on the counter. "Sorry! Hi. I like your dog."

Cole tamped down on a teeny, tiny jealous part of him. Leo hadn't taken to *Niamh* like that. Then again, Niamh was a familiar, not a pet, and talking animals were probably a bit of a shock. "Leo, Avery. Avery, this is Leo," he said. "He's a client. The flowers showed up at his place."

Avery gave Leo a once-over, and that teeny, tiny jealous part of Cole grew into a *small* jealous part. "Nice to meet you," Avery said, friendly but professional. "Are you in some kind of trouble?"

Leo's shoulders slumped. "That's what we're trying to find out."

Avery shook his head and touched the daffodil again. Cole swore he could see the water level in the vase sinking as the flower bloomed more fully. "I recognize the flowers—they came from here. But I don't remember selling them, and the vase—that's definitely not something I carry."

Too much lead in the glass, Cole thought. And too old, and definitely too enchanted to be sold somewhere that catered to mundanes.

"What do you mean, you don't remember selling them?" Leo frowned at Avery, then looked at Cole. "How does he not remember? Were they stolen?"

"It's a possibility," Cole admitted. "No security system?"

Avery shook his head. "Just the old-fashioned kind." He waggled his fingers as though to indicate the occult. "Didn't think I'd need more, in this town."

"You probably don't." But it did preclude catching the perpetrator on video. "I don't suppose the day's cash-out was off?"

"Actually, now that you mention it." Avery eyed the bouquet, then flipped through a spiral-bound notebook next to the register. "Yeah, I had extra. Approximately what I would've charged for a bouquet like that, but I didn't write it in my receipt book. See?" He handed the book over.

Leo took it before Cole could and held it close to his face, squinting. "Actually I think maybe you did write a receipt." He took a pen from the wire cup on the desk and poked at the torn-off bits of paper still stuck in the coils. "Looks like someone took your carbon copy."

Avery groaned. "My sister's going to give me so much shit for not switching over to digital when she bugged me about it."

Cole wasn't sure that wouldn't have resulted in a fried hard drive, but he kept mum.

"Why don't you remember, though?" Leo asked.

Cole and Avery exchanged glances. "Memory charm." The room seemed to dim a bit as Avery made the realization, and the flowers in the vase shriveled.

"Memory charm," Leo repeated. He looked at Cole, expression halfway between jaded and imploring. "That's not just a made-up thing from Harry Potter, I'm guessing."

"Sorry." This whole situation was a mess. Cole didn't blame Leo for feeling overwhelmed. But in the meantime, he had a suspicious occurrence to investigate. He turned back to Avery. "You want me to have a look?"

Avery shrugged. He didn't seem hopeful that Cole would find anything, but he didn't seem particularly concerned either. Maybe his kind had a sort of spidey sense for when they were in real danger. "Be my guest."

The remnants of the spell still clung to him, even through his own aura, though they were sloughing away. But Cole doubted even Avery's natural abilities would undo the work the charm had already done. "Well, it was definitely a spell. Not enough of it left to finger a suspect, though."

"It was worth a shot." Avery frowned at his receipt book, then set it aside. "It seems strange, doesn't it? Sending a protection bouquet with a cursed object?"

"It's definitely strange," Cole said grimly.

Something pawed at his leg, and he looked down and smiled at Tink, who was grinning up at him with her sweet pit bull smile and leaning on his leg as though she thought he needed a hug—or more likely, that she needed butt scritches. Cole obliged.

Leo sighed and knelt to pet her under the chin. "Now what?"

Cole knew where he had to go, but he couldn't take Leo with him. Not this time. Not yet. He let out a long, slow breath and prepared himself for the inevitable. "I'll drop you at my place. There's something I have to do alone."

Chapter Ten

"LOCK the door behind you," Kate said without looking up.

One day Cole was going to get used to that. It still made the hair on the back of his neck stand up. But he slid the dead bolt into place, and then he dropped into the chair across the desk. "So you've been expecting me."

For once, the desk was almost completely empty. Kate stuck her needles in whatever project she was working on and set it in the basket on the floor. "Kind of. Thought you might bring your guy."

"He's not my guy." He'd only known him a little over a week. And now they were roommates. He remembered mocking Leo for giving Roman a key too soon; the irony wasn't lost on him.

Kate didn't dignify that with a response. Instead she reached for the tarot deck sitting at the right-hand side of the desk and passed it across to him. "Shuffle."

The cards were really too big to shuffle the normal way, but Kate had worn this deck in over many years, and she'd been making Cole practice shuffling since she was old enough to have her own tarot. He shuffled, cut the deck, shuffled again for good measure. Then he passed them back.

Kate tapped the top card rhythmically. "So?"

Right. Cole ran a hand through his hair and willed his palms not to sweat. "Three-card spread," he decided. *Please let that be enough.* "What do I need to know about me and Leo?"

Kate flipped over the first card.

A boy facing left, holding a cup in one white-gloved hand: a willingness to take on evil. Cole often drew the Page of Cups.

"No surprise there," Kate said, and turned over the card that would represent Leo.

Four of Swords. Isolation. That made sense.

"Magically cockblocked." Kate raised an eyebrow. "Ready?"

Cole's stomach twisted. "No, but do it anyway."

The Wheel of Fortune.

Roaring filled Cole's ears, and his heart beat triple time. It could mean so many things. Time. The solution to a problem. "Destiny," he whispered, reaching out to trace a shaking finger down the side of the card.

Kate frowned at the deck and gathered the cards. "I thought you weren't going to break the curse the old-fashioned way," she grumbled, shuffling before fanning the cards on the table.

"I'm not!" Cole protested. "That card could mean anything."

Pursing her lips, Kate gestured to the table. "I should've made you ask a better question. We need information about who cursed Leo and what they want. What else he might be in danger from."

Cole sighed. "Yeah." This time he thought a moment before phrasing the question. "What do I need to do to protect him?"

He reached across the table and pulled a card from the fan: the Chariot. *Conflict. Turbulence. Searching for the truth.* Exactly what Cole might have expected of a card describing the situation. "Not exactly anything new there either."

"Shut up and draw again."

Past influences turned up the Hanged Man. "He really hurt that vampire's pride," Kate murmured, setting the card below and to the left of the Chariot.

"Yikes."

The Devil, inverted, took the place of the Future card. Cole stared at it for a moment, dumbfounded. "Divorce?" he guessed. Inverting the card changed the meaning. "That doesn't make any sense."

"Release from the ties that bind," Kate corrected, watching him with calculating eyes.

Cole squirmed. "I don't think that's—"

"I'm sorry, which of us is the clairvoyant, here?" she said sharply. He flinched. Kate went on more gently, "I know it's scary. I know it's new territory for you. Okay? But even if it weren't for this, even if Leo didn't need you, I know *you*. And you have wanted to fall in love your whole life."

Damn it. Closing his eyes, Cole concentrated on breathing in and out. His throat felt thick. Most days he put it out of his mind or made light of it as he had with Leo.

But sometimes he remembered he wasn't allowed to have what others took for granted. The universe wouldn't allow it.

"Cole, I'm sorry. I...."

He shook his head. "You didn't say anything that's not true." He opened his eyes again and met Kate's. "Come on. Two more cards. Next one's Reason, right?"

For a second he thought Kate would protest, try to comfort him further. But instead she gestured at the fanned-out cards and waited for Cole to select one.

Kate turned it over.

The High Priestess's eyes seemed to stare out from the card, impassive and judgmental. Cold. Superior. Cole had been on the receiving end of that stare enough times. Even the tarot card seemed to ooze power.

"That's the least surprising card we've turned over all session."

Having his suspicions confirmed didn't make Cole feel any better either. He slid the final card out from the fan and flipped it, done with the ritual of the thing. The Sun shone up at him, bright with promise of love, happiness, fulfillment, health, all if he did what the cards asked. If he broke the curse the old-fashioned way.

"Well," Kate said awkwardly. "No pressure." Then she made a face at herself as she started gathering up the cards. "I'm sorry. I shouldn't have pushed. I—"

"It's fine," Cole cut her off. "At least we learned *something*." That their suspicions were well-founded. That Leo's ex was a piece of work. And that if he wanted to keep Leo safe, one way or another, he had to break the curse.

"Still, I could've been—"

And then a weird thing happened: Kate fumbled the deck.

In all the years Cole had known her—which amounted to his entire life—he'd never once seen her mishandle the cards. Now, though, as she was putting them together in a pile, one slipped out from the bundle, teetered on the edge of the desk, and finally fell to the floor.

Cole didn't dare look. "If you had to guess, what does that card represent, do you think?"

"If I had to guess?" she repeated. Her skin had taken on an unusual pallor. "Consequences. What happens if you don't release Leo from the curse."

"You know what card it is, don't you."

"There's really only one it could be."

Cole nodded. Then, steeling himself, he peered over the edge of the desk.

On the floor, half-hidden under the desk, lay the Tower, cracked down the middle, burning, its former occupants crashing to their deaths.

Destiny, Cole thought grimly. Okay.

Chapter Eleven

LEO felt more normal once he'd put on his own clothes. A little snooping led him to the laundry room, and he left the sweats and T-shirt he'd borrowed there, conscious of his tendency to leave things on the floor.

"I guess I'm your new roommate," he told Niamh, who was preening a wing on her perch.

"As long as you don't leave the toilet seat up."

"I'll try to remember, I—" A squawk of laughter interrupted him. *I'm talking to a bird. And she's making fun of me. Surreal.*

He didn't want to know whether she used the toilet. Instead, he set about looking for something useful to do. He'd had a roommate in Toronto, but they'd mostly worked opposite shifts. Leo rarely saw her; they accomplished most of their communication via Post-it notes stuck to the fridge, largely about which food was up for grabs and which was not.

Speaking of food—"Do you think Cole will be back for lunch?"

Niamh finished preening and cocked her head. It was a disconcertingly human mannerism. "Hard to say. Any other day he'd probably go to work after visiting Kate, but I think he's worried about you."

Just what Leo needed. His stomach squirmed with guilt. He wanted to protest that he could take care of himself, except both he and the bird knew he couldn't. Not in this strange new world.

He can always heat it up if he's not home in time. Making lunch would give Leo something productive to do and hopefully serve as a preliminary thank-you. As he strode toward the kitchen, he called over his shoulder, "So does this happen a lot? People needing to crash here because of whatever curse Cole's supposed to break?"

Niamh flapped over and alit on the back of a kitchen chair. "No. You're the first."

That probably meant he was super fucked. Not a great feeling. Leo opened the fridge to take inventory. "Really? I would have thought...." He hadn't thought his case was special. Hell, he hadn't wanted it to be.

"Cole's good at what he does. He doesn't brag, but witches talk. People know him."

"Yeah, makes sense." After all, Victoria had known where to send him. He wondered if she was still doing that thing in Thailand. Maybe he should try to FaceTime her. "So then what?" he asked, riffling through the deli drawer. Promising.

"What do you mean, then what? He breaks the curse and they go home."

Leo paused with his hand around a package of cheese. "Like, right away?"

When he turned around, Niamh had frozen with her right foot halfway to her beak. Had she frozen because grooming in the kitchen was objectively disgusting or because she'd given away more about Leo's curse than she intended? "Sometimes they go home while Cole gathers ingredients to break the spell."

"Guess I'm just *special*." But pouting about it wouldn't improve his situation. Lunch, on the other hand—well, at least his stomach would stop grumbling. He pulled out a package of bacon and a jar of mayo. "Where did Cole go, anyway?"

"His cousin Kate runs a magic shop in town."

Leo frowned, pulling open random kitchen drawers. Surely even a witch needed kitchen scissors—there, in the wooden cylinder with all the spatulas. "There's no magic shop in town."

"Magic shop slash yarn store," Niamh corrected.

Of course. Leo took a heavy-bottomed frying pan from the rack hanging above the stove. "I guess a town this small wouldn't be able to support a magic shop."

Niamh squawked sharply. "Shows what you know."

Leo wished he hadn't said anything. Now he was torn between curiosity and terror. He put the bacon in the pan, wondering if asking for clarification would make the situation worse.

Niamh didn't give him the option. She sighed. "It's the land here, and the water. Look, do you know much about water? Energy?"

"Not in the way I think you mean." He paused. He hadn't brought that many clothes, and bacon grease tended to spatter. Then he remembered what Cole had said at the festival. "Is there an apron somewhere?"

Niamh indicated the pantry. "There, back of the door."

"Thanks."

As he put it on, Niamh continued, "Water, fresh water, is something almost everything on the planet needs to survive. Because of that, fresh water contains a sort of energy. And the Great Lakes contain 21 percent of the world's supply."

Leo turned the knob to medium heat. "Okay. That much I think I remember from elementary school geography class. But Lake Erie's the smallest lake, right? Or almost."

Niamh fluttered her wings. "Gold star. Lake Erie's the second-smallest by surface area but the shallowest by far."

"So why not camp out around Lake Superior?"

"Oh, we do. Those of us who don't mind the cold, that is." Fair point. "But think of it as a giant funnel. Superior, Huron, Michigan—all that water, all that *power* is heading to the Atlantic."

"And Lake Erie is the bottom of the funnel. Well, Niagara Falls. I guess that makes sense." The bacon started to pop, and Leo remembered he still hadn't found a suitable utensil. "What about Lake Ontario, though?" Before she could answer, it came to him. "I guess it's deep enough that it's more like a second funnel."

"In the thing with the spatula," Niamh suggested. "Right of the stove. And yes, that's the basic idea."

Leo snagged the tongs and prodded at the pan. "So if I wanted to avoid vampires and witches and—I don't know what other creatures of the night are out there, don't tell me—I should move to the desert."

"Ha! Deserts have their own power." She rustled again, audible above the ever-more-frequent cracks of bacon fat. "Why are you so afraid, anyway?"

Sharply, Leo raised his head and narrowed his eyes at her. "I don't know, maybe because my ex-boyfriend *cursed me*? Sorry if that doesn't exactly endear the—the *community* to me."

Niamh twitched, ruffling her feathers and then smoothing them. "Okay, that's reasonable. But we're not more criminal than anyone else, you know."

An icy chill washed down Leo's back. The idea that Cole might think Leo was afraid of him made his gut twist. "I'm not…. I'm adjusting to this world where all of a sudden people have abilities I didn't think were possible, and some of them are dangerous and I'm helpless to defend myself. I'm not *used* to that." If someone pointed a gun at him, at least he could duck. He didn't have the first idea how to avoid being cursed, other than not to touch strange objects without cotton gloves.

At a loss for what else to say, he flipped over a piece of bacon. A drop of grease spattered on his wrist, and he hissed.

"Hmm." Niamh's talons click-scritched on the back of the chair as she hopped closer. "Maybe I could help you."

"What?"

She jumped to the next chair, the one closest to Leo. "You can't identify obscures on sight. You don't know how to protect yourself. But if you have a suspicion, I could give you a signal. People don't notice birds."

"They do if they're indoors," Leo pointed out, but it was a weak protest. "That's really kind of you. Thanks."

"Well." Niamh craned her neck around and preened the feathers on her back. "Any friend of Cole's." Then she swiveled and cocked her head again. "Are you going to eat all that bacon?"

COLE opened his front door to the mouthwatering scent
of frying bacon. For a second he stood in the entryway,
overcome with longing. He couldn't remember the last
time he'd come home to a cooked meal, but it must
have been before he moved out of Gran's house. He let
himself have one short, involved moment of self-pity,
because today had sucked and he'd earned it.

Then he told himself getting emotional over pork
was extra even for him. "Honey, I'm home," he called,
surprised when the words came out without issue. "And
you cooked!" He toed off his shoes and made his way
to the kitchen.

"I fried bacon," Leo corrected, smiling from behind
the counter. He had changed into his own clothes—not
that the tight T-shirt and jeans concealed his body any
more than Cole's had—and put on Cole's apron over
them so his chest read I'm Kind of a Big Dill. Cole's
heart tried to beat its way out of his chest. "I figured
we could have BLTs on the bagels left over from this
morning. What's another six hundred calories when
you're breaking curses, right?"

Cole's mouth watered. "Right," he agreed, taking
deep breaths through his nose. "What is that smell?"
Beneath the bacon lurked something sweet and earthy.

"Oh! You only had cherry tomatoes for the BLTs.
Kind of awkward to put on sandwiches—they tend to slip
out. So I candied them in the oven. Now they're soft."

Even without the curse holding him back, Cole
couldn't have articulated a response to that. Leo had
turned healthy food into candy—for him. "Can I help?"
he offered after a too-long pause.

"Nah, they're done. But you can eat."

They sat across from each other at the kitchen table, Cole thankful he had food to distract him. After everything Kate had said—after what the *cards* had said—he wanted to hide upstairs and lick his wounds. Or at least he had *thought* he'd want that. But now, actually sitting across from Leo, their feet almost touching under the table, he could almost forget.

The sandwich didn't hurt.

"Oh my God," Cole accidentally exclaimed around a mouthful of bacon and tomato. He closed his eyes, chewed, swallowed, savoring the smoky salt of the bacon and the warm juicy pop of sweet cherry tomato. He pulled the bagel away from his mouth and licked his lips before raising his eyes to meet Leo's. "Are you sure you're not magic?"

"Pretty sure." Leo licked a drop of tomato juice off his thumb. Cole's mouth watered, and it had nothing to do with the food. "But I can google with the best of them."

"Clearly."

They didn't talk much until they'd finished eating the sandwiches—and then polished off the extra tomatoes as well. Cole was wiping his fingers on a napkin when Leo asked, "So what were you doing at your cousin's?"

Cole blinked.

"Niamh told me where you went." She must have gone out for a flight afterward, because the kitchen window was open and her perch was empty. Trying to give them some privacy, maybe. All the women in Cole's family were nosy meddlers. "Did you get what you needed at your cousin's shop?"

He huffed out a laugh. *Funny you should ask that.* "In a manner of speaking."

"Do you have a big family?" Leo asked, standing to put the plates in the dishwasher. "You mentioned your cousin Kate and your cousin Julie and your grandmother and your mother...."

Cole rose too and grabbed the frying pan and baking sheet to wash by hand. "You seem to have hit on the theme of the family, at least."

"Not a lot of boys in the family tree?"

"I'm the Alpin black sheep." He paused and frowned at the idiom. "More of a light brown, I guess, but all my mom's siblings are women, and all my cousins, and all their kids. Well, except my stepnephew, but his bio mom's not an Alpin."

Leo closed the dishwasher and cocked his hip against the counter, smiling. "How's that work, then?"

With all of that to look at, Cole found it a little difficult to concentrate. "Magic, probably. We're a strong matriarchy, of course. My grandmother's grandmother settled here in the 1800s. Never would take a man's name. Insisted he take hers."

"In the 1800s?" Leo said, raising his eyebrows. "I would have liked to meet her."

"Me too," Cole admitted, plugging the sink to fill it with hot water. "I might've, if she'd lived much longer. I think she was 114 when she died."

Leo cocked his head and studied Cole carefully. "I bet you take after her."

Cole blushed and turned back to the pan. "Anyway. She settled here because of the strong magic in the water. Family legend has it she appointed herself one of the lake's guardians—typical white person, right? Appoint yourself the guardian after you forced the land's real caretakers out of the best areas? But anyway, now nobody ever dares leave." He paused in picking up the sponge. "Well, almost nobody."

Leo pulled the dish towel from the front of the oven and stood waiting with it while Cole scrubbed the bacon from the bottom of the pan. "Sounds like there's a story there."

"My mom," Cole admitted. "If I'm the black sheep of the Alpin family, I guess she's the red one. I didn't meet my dad till I was nine, but Gran's house was plenty full when I was growing up, and Mom, well." He smiled fondly and rinsed the pan before handing it over. "She was an Alpin, and nobody was going to tell her what to do. Not even Gran."

"Why do I feel like those words lead to trouble?"

"I would think it's probably obvious." Cole shook his head thinking of different times—the Samhains and Solstices, the backyard gatherings. Monarch butterflies flocking as he and his mother danced barefoot in the autumn sunshine. "Mom met a man. American. Of course she did, she was beautiful—still is."

Leo finished drying the pot and set it down on the counter as Cole washed the baking sheet. "Let me guess: Gran didn't approve."

"Gran didn't approve," Cole confirmed, rinsing the suds away. "I never heard the full argument, so I can only guess what hurtful things were said. At the end of it, Mom told me to pack my bags, and we were going to go live in Florida with Geoff, and didn't I want to go to Disney World?"

For a moment Leo said nothing, though he spent an inordinate amount of time ensuring he'd absorbed every drop of moisture from the baking sheet. "And did you want to go to Disney World?"

"I wanted to go wherever my mother was. I adored her." He still did, even if time and distance and Gran had strained their relationship. "And I did, eventually, but only to visit. I never found out what Gran told her, but she…." His throat tightened and didn't loosen again until Leo swayed close enough to bump his hip against Cole's. "She told me the plan had changed, and it would be better for me here. So I stayed here with Gran during the school year, and I'd spend summer and winter breaks in Orlando." He managed a smile. "Mom still takes me to Disney World every year."

"I'm sorry," Leo said quietly. "That sounds hard."

"It does sound a bit sordid when I put it that way," Cole covered, feeling raw. "But I grew up with Kate and Julie and my other cousins, running wild at family parties on Samhain and Beltane, and I never lacked for anything. And after Mom left, I guess Gran must have felt bad, because she tracked down my dad and introduced us." The name Marcel Costa wouldn't mean anything to Leo, but anyone who'd grown up in town would know the family, Brazilian immigrants who'd started a greenhouse enterprise. "He was pretty cautious at first. I think he heard the rumors about the family and was afraid of Mom and Gran."

"Sensible guy," Leo commented.

Cole snorted in acknowledgment. "Yeah. It was nice getting to know him, though. Made me feel a lot better about maybe not having magic. He's busy with work and his family—he married when I was fifteen—but I see them at Christian holidays." And they accepted that Cole's family were "pagan" and didn't care that he was gay except to bug him about when he was going to bring a boyfriend to Easter dinner for the kids to pick on.

That thought led nowhere good, though, so he shook his head, redirecting the conversation. "What's your family like?"

"Small and undramatic." Leo shrugged, hanging the dish towel back where he'd taken it from. "My parents are both only children, and it's just us and my sister. My parents retired to Florida too, actually. And my sister's on a golf scholarship in South Carolina."

"That's awesome for her." Cole could do with more female athletes getting scholarships. "Sounds like it might be lonely for you, though."

A fleeting smile faded across Leo's face. "Good guess."

You won't be lonely here, Cole wanted to promise, but the words wouldn't come out. And he couldn't reach out either, too raw. "I—"

Niamh alit on the kitchen window. "Don't suppose you saved me any bacon?"

Leo turned away to fetch it, and the moment broke. Ten minutes later Cole escaped to the privacy of his shop, the weight of the universe's expectations heavy on his heart.

Chapter Twelve

LEO started the midnight shift Monday, so at least his first week with a roommate should be fairly painless, since they wouldn't be in each other's pockets. He and Cole stayed up until eleven critiquing *Dancing with the Stars* contestants on Saturday; then Cole went to bed and Leo binged *Breaking Bad* on Netflix. Talk about giving him perspective.

He woke too early on Monday to the sound of "Single Ladies: the Cole Alpin Remix." He stared at the ceiling for a minute, wondering if he should say something, but going upstairs and interrupting Cole's shower concert seemed like a lot of effort. Besides, it was kind of funny, and he could always go back to sleep when Cole had left.

He yawned intermittently all day, but that wasn't unusual for the first day of a swing shift.

"Coffee," Jimmy said at two, handing over a mug. "You look like you need it."

Leo snorted but took the cup. "Start an IV." An old joke, but who could come up with fresh material at this hour?

Despite the time, he managed to remember to drive back to Cole's rather than his own place, and he stumbled blearily up the stairs and into the shower before falling face-first onto the couch and passing out.

He'd been asleep what felt like ten minutes—the insides of his eyelids were still grainy—when the water kicked on upstairs. Groaning, he pressed his face into his pillow. So living with a roommate while working midnights was going to require some adjustments. He made a mental note to buy a sleep mask and some noise-canceling headphones and reminded himself Cole didn't owe him anything.

Still. It was going to be a long week.

THE clamor of the pipes shuddering to life woke Cole out of a dead sleep early Saturday morning, just as they had the rest of the week. He might as well get up and make coffee.

Except, when he got downstairs and filled the kettle, there wasn't any more coffee.

Cole stared at the empty bag, betrayed. Then he double-checked the pantry. Sadly, no life-giving little baggies of roasted goodness lurked on the shelves. The french press sat on the counter, a centimeter of water covering some slushy grinds. The grinder yielded nothing more promising than a few sad half-masticated beans.

Cole had promised Danielle the day off in exchange for her handling last Friday, or he would have climbed back up the stairs and put himself back to bed. Maybe he could put up a sign saying he was out sick and the store would be closed today? But Saturdays were good business days. Or maybe—

"Hey." Leo entered the living room, moving as if his feet were tied together and he was fighting gravity for every step.

"Did you drink the last of the coffee?" Cole blurted.

Leo stopped in his tracks, mouth open. "I—shit. Yeah." He rubbed his eyes, grimacing. "Sorry. I meant to grab more before work, but I've been a little...."

"Distracted?" Cole suggested, deflating a little. It seemed mean to get confrontational when Leo was dealing with a lot.

"Exhausted." Now that he mentioned it, Cole noticed the dark circles under his eyes and the pallor to his skin. Maybe the midnight shift didn't agree with him? Or he was having nightmares? Or—"I wake up every time you shower, and it's a lot harder to fall back asleep when it's light outside."

Oooooor Cole had unwittingly been a bad roommate too. "Oh." This was awkward. "Sorry." Then, "Why didn't you say anything?"

Leo gave a twisted, aborted shrug. "You're already helping me break a curse, plus I'm sleeping on your couch, watching your TV, using your internet, drinking your coffee.... Complaining about your shower karaoke routine seemed ungrateful."

Oh God. Cole's ears burned. "All right. Well. I'll cancel the morning edition while you're on midnights. And I'm calling a plumber, because the rattling pipes wake me up every time *you* shower."

Leo tossed the couch cushions onto the floor and gave a laugh that turned into a groan. "We are going to have to communicate better. I'll shower at work when I'm on midnights. You don't have to go to the trouble."

"Maybe not, but I should probably have them checked out anyway before they explode and we have to start taking sponge baths in the kitchen sink." And now he should change the subject before things got awkward, because Leo was climbing into bed and Cole was talking about being naked, and that combination couldn't go anywhere fun. "I'll grab a coffee on my way into the shop. You look done in."

"Thanks." Leo pulled the sheet up and closed his eyes.

Cole had been debating getting out the Swiffer to clear up the dust bunnies in the corner, but he decided it could wait.

"SO we're still on for tomorrow night, right?" Amy asked, putting her credit card back in her purse as Cole finished packing up that week's order.

Leo set Cole's lunch on the counter of the candy shop and then froze. He'd run into Amy by accident, but it was a good thing he had, because he'd forgotten he'd agreed to host games night, thinking that the curse would be broken and he'd be back in his own place by now. "Oh my God, I totally forgot. My apartment's being fumigated." He hoped he hid his wince at the lie. Just when he was getting the hang of being a better roommate…. "I've been staying with Cole. Hence the lunch delivery. Least I could do."

Cole peered into the bag, then laughed. "This is a sandwich from Tim Hortons."

"A sandwich *and* a donut," Leo corrected, faux defensive. "I was out running errands and didn't have time to go ho—back to your place first." Jeez. He'd been there two weeks. Maybe he was getting a little too comfortable.

"Well, I won't complain," Cole said, pulling out the donut. He looked at it the way guys in the club used to look at Leo. Should he give them a moment?

Before he could make a comment, Cole put the donut down—carefully, so only the paper touched the counter. "Anyway, you can have games night at my place if you want. I don't mind."

Keenly aware of Amy's shrewd gaze, Leo asked, "You're sure? You're already doing me a huge favor…."

Cole shrugged. "I don't have any plans Saturday night, barring maybe some Netflix."

"Do you like games?" Amy broke in, sweet as the rock candy in the jar on the counter. "We can always use one more player."

Leo fought the urge to stomp on her foot. After two weekly games nights—he'd missed one because of work—he knew more of those games had adult themes than not, and he couldn't guarantee the curse wouldn't keep him from flirting with Cole, even within the context of a game. Because he was starting to *mean* it.

Meaning it hadn't exactly worked out well for him last time. Besides, he liked winning.

"I wouldn't want to intrude—"

"Nonsense! In your own house?" Amy pished. "I'll bring wine. You bring your A game."

Cole smiled, obviously pleased to be included, damn it, which meant Leo didn't have the heart to try to talk him out of it. "Oh, I will. See you tomorrow."

"I, um, I'm gonna go too," Leo said. "See you at your place?"

"Sure."

"Amy, you want to get a coffee?" he asked, perhaps a bit desperately.

"Didn't you just come from Tim Hortons?" Amy asked, unfortunately before the shop door closed behind them.

Leo's face flamed. Now Cole probably thought Leo wanted to talk to Amy about *him*, and—he hadn't realized how much not being able to flirt directly would make him feel like a seventh grader. "Yes, but not for *coffee*." Timmies' baked goods and sandwiches were tasty, but he didn't drink their dishwater brew. Not when he could go to Caffeine.

"Uh-huh," Amy said, but she looped her arm through his and allowed him to lead her across the street. "So fumigation, eh? How lucky you've managed to find another friend in town."

Her tone was teasing but also probing. Leo didn't need any more questions right now. He was having a hard enough time being honest with himself. "I promise I'm sleeping on the couch."

"Oh, all right," she said, scooting inside the café when he held the door for her. "But you have to admit, he's pretty cute, right?"

Did Leo have to admit that? The blush he could feel heating his cheeks seemed to think so. "He wouldn't normally have been my type," he admitted as they got into line. Cole was too sunny, too open, too genuine.

"But?"

Damn her, she was just too perceptive. Maybe she had obscure powers after all. "But my normal type turned out to be 'douchebag.'" At least that made them easy to get over.

Amy laughed and let Leo buy her a coffee, and they found a table in the back corner.

"So what's the latest on the wedding you're coordinating?"

"All set. A total of three hours on the phone and a few emails sent and they're all set for December 21." She shrugged and held her mug close to her face. "If they were all that easy I could take a week's vacation every month."

"The dream," Leo teased.

"Oh, don't give me that. You *could*, you lucky thing."

"Yeah, but I'd end up working ten days back-to-back." He'd done it before, but it made him feel like the walking dead.

Shit, he hoped the walking dead weren't a real thing.

"True." Amy took a sip and set her drink down. "And it's no fun to take a week off and go on vacation by yourself. Or at least it would get old after a few months. I like some company."

Leo nodded. "Yeah, I think I'd get sick of myself." It would be nice to go visit his parents, maybe. He hadn't seen much of them since last Christmas, and this year he'd be low on the seniority list and would probably have to work. Maybe he could visit in January instead, make it a New Year's thing.

"Maybe I'll go away in March," Amy mused. "Hardly anyone gets married in March."

"You'll jinx it," Leo warned, and then wondered if *that* was real.

He needed to get a handle on himself.

"Not strategizing for tomorrow night, are you?"

Leo looked up and smiled. Andre, the café owner, stood beside their table, smiling impishly—not literally impishly, Leo didn't think, though the smooth pale skin and dimples certainly *could* have belonged to an imp. If Leo's mental image of imps was accurate. But he was pretty sure six four was too tall. "That's cheating," Andre added.

Amy kicked out a chair for him and he sat. "We haven't even drawn teams yet. And anyway we've got a new player tomorrow because Leo's apartment's being fumigated."

Andre cocked his head, a smooth, elegant gesture. "You're over in the place on Main Street, aren't you? I have a friend who lives in that building. I'm surprised he didn't mention anything."

Damn small towns. Did everyone always have to know everyone else? "It's just my place with the problem, I guess," Leo lied, hoping he didn't sound completely transparent. "Honestly, I stopped listening when they started talking about bugs. I'm happier not knowing."

Amy shivered. "Don't blame you."

"So we're meeting at your place again?" Andre asked her.

"Um, no." Leo smiled. "That's… my friend Cole is putting me up until I can go back to my place. He volunteered to let us have game night there so Amy doesn't have to clean two Saturdays in a row."

Amy wadded up her napkin and threw it at him.

"Actually, maybe he just wanted me to vacuum?" Leo joked aloud, snatching the paper out of the air. "I would've done it anyway."

"Well, I look forward to tomorrow's victory," Andre joked. Then he tapped his palm flat on the table twice and stood smoothly. "See you then. I have to go sling coffee. One of my baristas has the flu."

Amy shook her head and then checked her watch. "Shoot, I have to go too. I have a meeting with a vendor at one. You going to be all right?"

What an odd question. Unless she knew something? "I'll be fine," Leo promised. "I've drunk caffeine unsupervised before, I promise."

She stuck her tongue out. "See you tomorrow, then."

Once they'd left, Leo sat in his seat at the table in the corner, watching the people in the café. If Niamh was right, some of the people in here belonged in Cole's world, not his. Or—no, that wasn't right. They had as much right to this world as Leo, only they experienced it in a completely different way.

What else might be real? Leo wondered. Talking magpies. Witches. Vampires. Leprechauns, maybe? Banshees? Sea monsters? Demons?

What about goblins? That woman sitting near the window looked furtive, the way she was shoving that cookie in her mouth. Did goblins like cookies? Or was that an elf thing?

Never mind. Whichever it was, Leo and Cole didn't have any, and you couldn't host a successful games night without snacks. Leo needed to go shopping.

COLE spent Saturday morning at the shop, making candy. It helped take his mind off… things, with Leo, like the way Leo had looked first thing when Cole got up, passed out on Cole's couch, shirtless and with the blanket tangled around his legs.

He would've looked better in Cole's bed.

Torn between tucking the blanket around him properly and not wanting Leo to wake up while Cole was doing something so sappy, he'd left well enough alone. Leo sat up while Cole was making coffee, stretched so languidly that Cole spilled grounds all over the counter, and then offered a sleepy smile.

Cole needed the complete meditation of candymaking today. He immersed himself in sugar and flavor, color and texture. By the time three o'clock rolled around, he'd made raspberry-basil candy sticks the same blue as Leo's eyes, apricot pastilles the exact shade of Leo's hair, and very pink, plump bubblegum.

So apparently Cole's subconscious was having some thoughts at work. It happened. Or at least he was pretty sure it happened to other people, though he'd never experienced it himself until now. He bagged some of the candy to take home to games night, waved at Danielle, who was entertaining a group of kids with party hats, and left the shop.

Strains of music drifted out the open windows as he pulled into his driveway. Curious, he listened for a minute, wondering about Leo's taste in music. After their talk a week ago, Leo had been on very good roommate behavior, and he hadn't played anything loud enough to be overheard. Cole had expected hip-hop, R&B, the sort of music played at the clubs Leo had frequented until recently. Instead he got the Shangri-Las. Cute.

Inside the front door, Cole started to kick off his shoes—and then stopped and looked around. Leo must have been as busy as Cole this morning, because the house gleamed. The hardwood floors looked like they'd just been polished. The air smelled of lemons. The baseboards shone. The air held not a single speck of dust.

Cole bent over and untied his shoes, then put them in the front closet, which had also had a face-lift. "Leo?" Jeez, he'd even washed Niamh's perch. *Cole* hated that job, even though Niamh never left a mess in the house. The feathers made him sneeze.

"Hey," Leo said from the kitchen. "Come here and taste this?"

Cole turned toward him to find him standing only a few inches away, holding a spoonful of something warm and fragrant to Cole's mouth, his other hand cupped beneath as if to prevent drips. The warmth of him radiated through the space between them. Half a step and Cole could close the gap. And part of him yearned to. Would Leo back away? Or would he let Cole into his space? What would he feel like in Cole's arms? What would his kiss taste like?

Leo must have blinked, or something, because suddenly Cole remembered he was supposed to be doing something. Something besides staring intently, potentially making his houseguest uncomfortable. His houseguest who didn't have anywhere else safe to go, Cole reminded himself. And the universe didn't intend Leo for him. No perving. "Uh," he said intelligently, "there's no hazelnuts in that, right? I'm allergic and my EpiPen is in the car."

"No hazelnuts," Leo promised. Was his voice a little husky? What had Leo been cooking to make the kitchen so warm?

With nothing intelligent to say, Cole opened his mouth. Leo nudged the spoon into it.

Warm, gooey, tangy flavor melted on Cole's tongue, and without meaning to, he chased the spoon as Leo withdrew it. He wanted to get every last drop of cheesy goodness. And then the note of spice hit him and he hummed in surprise.

Or he meant to. It might, judging by the wide-eyed, lips-parted startlement on Leo's face, have come out as a moan.

Leo cleared his throat. "Good?" he prompted. His cheeks flamed, and his eyes seemed a particularly luminous blue.

"Yeah, yes, that's...." Cole licked his lips. "What is that, some kind of dip... thing?"

"Warm artichoke dip." Leo hadn't moved back yet. He was watching Cole's mouth.

Cole was melting like chocolate in the sun. "That's nice." He needed to think of something else to say, something to break the tension between them. Otherwise he was going to lean forward and—"Is something on fire?"

The pleasant color fled Leo's face. "Oh shit!" He spun around and used the dip spoon to pick up a paper towel that had been left too close to the burner and started smoldering. Leo dropped both items into the kitchen sink just as the paper towel went up in flames. He rushed to turn the water on while Cole shut off the burner.

"Well," Leo said sheepishly, "now I remember why I don't usually cook."

Cole prodded at an ashen piece of paper towel with a knife. It disintegrated on the stovetop. Oh well. Cleanup wouldn't take too long, at least. "Tendency to get distracted?"

"Usually I have Niamh to supervise, and she keeps me on task." He turned the water off and pulled a soggy, singed paper glob out of the sink. "She's mostly interested in the food, but she makes sure I don't burn anything too. I never really cook when it's just me—too much work."

Niamh must be out for her afternoon social with the other neighborhood familiars. But Cole wasn't going to tell Leo that. Not yet. Maybe soon. "Well, no permanent harm done."

"I'm sorry. I can't believe I...."

He trailed off, and Cole looked at him. Couldn't believe he what? His ears were still red, and he was looking at his feet. *Can't believe I spoon-fed you? Can't believe we almost kissed?*

"Don't worry about it." Cole smiled. "At least you didn't get sugar on the burner. I've done that a time or three hundred. It's a pain in the ass to clean up, *and* it stinks. This is no big deal."

"This is the last thing I needed to get ready anyway." Leo shooed Cole away from the stove. "I'll clean this up, and then we'll be set." He glanced at the clock on the microwave. "Of course, that still leaves four hours to kill before everyone gets here."

Cole could think of six or seven hundred ways to fill those hours, but the last time he'd let things get too heated, something literally caught on fire. Talk about signs from the universe. Probably best that he put some distance between them until he regained his equilibrium. "Well, I have sugar…." He held up his hands to demonstrate, though Leo probably couldn't see the granules clinging to Cole unless he had superpowers. "Pretty much everywhere, actually. So I'm gonna go shower and then"—*don't say it*—"have a nap. You going to brush up on your drawing skills for Pictionary?"

"I'm much better at the interpretation side of Pictionary," Leo said. "Years of practice reading doctors' handwriting, probably."

The moment started to draw out again. Cole needed to get out of this kitchen. "All right, well." He clamped down on the urge to rub the back of his neck. He'd only end up feeling stickier and looking awkward to boot. "Let me know if anything else catches fire."

Chapter Thirteen

NATURALLY, Amy was the first to arrive, a bag of wine in one hand and a stack of games balanced precariously in the other.

"Hey, let me get those before they fall," Leo said, carefully relieving her of the boxes while Cole grabbed the wine and her coat. Charlotte and Grace followed from Amy's car and introduced themselves to Cole while Leo was setting up in the living room.

"Sorry, I know we're a little early," Amy said sheepishly.

"Party planner habit," chorused Leo and the couple she'd brought along with her, just as Amy said it herself.

Laughter followed, and Cole said bemusedly, "These people know you."

"Anyway, I don't mind being early," said Charlotte, already following Leo toward the living room. "It means we get to sample the goods before Andre eats it all. Show me the way!"

Andre showed up at twenty past, by which time Charlotte and Grace had eaten half the artichoke dip and Leo had guiltily consumed two raspberry-basil candy sticks rather than proper food. He might have to rethink his stance on candy.

It had started to rain, so Leo hurried to the door, but Andre seemed unperturbed, just letting the water run down his face. "Sorry I'm late."

"Believe it or not, we anticipated that." Leo smiled. For someone who ran his own business, Andre had a difficult time appearing anywhere on time. "Come on in out of the wet. I'll grab you a towel. I think Charlotte left you a pita chip or two."

Andre shook himself like a dog before stepping inside, leaving his soggy boots on the mat by the door, then looking around the house as if in wonder. Maybe he was checking all the doorways were tall enough for him to get through without ducking.

Four hours later Leo decided that Cranium was terrible and he should throw it in Lake Erie. And if Amy didn't stop laughing, he'd throw her in too.

His face burned. His ears burned. His whole *body* burned wherever Cole was touching him, which was a lot of places. Because right now he was acting as Cole's puppet while Cole tried to get him to guess the phrase written on the card.

Leo couldn't have made a decent guess if he'd had the card in front of him. He'd probably forgotten how to read. Cole had put him on his hands and knees on the carpet, while Cole knelt close—*very* close—behind him, making grasping motions at Leo's groin. Leo had never been so acutely aware of how long it had been since he last had sex.

"Time," Amy finally called, wiping away tears of laughter.

Cole sat back on his heels, and Leo let out what he hoped was a quiet sigh of relief. "What the hell was that?" he asked to cover, hoping it came out exasperated instead of flustered. Where was the curse to save him from *that*?

"Milking the cow!" Cole and Amy chorused. Amy went on, "Though have you ever seen anyone milk a cow? Here's a hint: don't stand behind the cow unless you want to get kicked."

Cole made a face at her. "Feel free to do better!"

Leo picked himself off the floor and handed Andre the die. "She has to wait her turn." He passed the die to Andre, who was still hiccupping with repressed laughter. "I hope you get green, you tone-deaf bastard."

By the end of the night, Leo was buzzing pleasantly from wine and good company. He and Cole waved goodbye to their guests at the door. Amy, Charlotte, and Grace hurried to the car, each holding a board game over their head, but Andre just put on his (still wet) boots and declined the offer of a ride to trudge home in the wet.

"I don't get him," Leo said, shaking his head as he closed the door and locked it. But when he looked up and met Cole's gaze, he found him too close, for maybe the hundredth time that day. Or maybe not close enough. Leo could admit that he'd initiated his share of those close encounters. But that was as far as it could go. The curse held him fast.

"He's an odd duck," Cole agreed with the hint of a smile. "Get it? Because he likes the rain?"

"Oh my God," Leo said, and got stuck on *I can't believe I like you so much*. He blushed anyway. Cole would probably blame the alcohol.

"Aww, come on. It was funny."

Leo smiled in spite of himself, but he couldn't hold Cole's gaze. "I'm, ah, I'm gonna go clean up." He chanced a glance at Cole, who looked almost like he was holding his breath. Leo swallowed. "You go on to bed. This was my thing, so…."

"I had fun too," Cole protested gently. "I don't mind helping."

Leo needed time to process. "It's your house," he said. "And you spent half the day at work before this. It's the least I can do."

Cole held his gaze for a few more endless seconds before he yawned and forfeited the argument. "Sorry," he said ruefully. "I guess I'll take you up on that. Good night."

"Good night," Leo whispered.

On autopilot, he went through a mental checklist for cleaning up: gathering dishes, loading them into the dishwasher, straightening the cushions. He opened the door to Cole's office and retrieved Niamh's perch, though she must have taken advantage of the open window to do some exploring. That made her as much of an odd duck as Andre, as far as Leo was concerned.

His brain kept buzzing into more and more dangerous territory, so he took the dishes out of the dishwasher again and filled the sink. Spoons and forks first. He cleaned them perhaps more thoroughly than necessary, staring out the kitchen window into the night.

Leo had always maintained that he dated so much because he was looking for love. And he'd believed that. But perhaps it hadn't been true.

He picked up a wineglass and submerged it in the water.

He could see now what he hadn't before. He'd spent his life pushing men away the second they got close. Oh, not all of them—he and Roman certainly wouldn't have worked out in the long run, that much was clear. But the others?

Water splashed onto the floor when he rinsed the glass, and a tapping on the window almost made him drop it. He put it down and threw up the sash.

"What're you doing penance for?" Niamh asked, hopping from the sill to the countertop, leaving a tiny trail of puddles behind her. "Doing dishes by hand after eleven on Saturday night?"

Leo sloshed at a dessert plate.

"Uh-oh." Niamh flapped over to a kitchen chair. "That was an ominous silence."

Leo huffed and set the plate in the drainer without rinsing it. Then he spun around and faced her. "Have you ever thought something about yourself, really believed it, and then one day you realized you've been lying to yourself?"

Niamh twitched a tailfeather. "How much wine did you drink?"

Leo made a face and picked up another dessert plate. "It's not the wine." Not just the wine, at least.

"Then I don't know what kind of party games you were playing, but I'm glad I wasn't invited."

He set the plate on the drainer, then gave it up and dropped into the chair across from Niamh. "I am afraid of love," he declared.

Perhaps Niamh knew rolling beady eyes wouldn't have much effect, because she rolled her entire head. "Please. You and every other fool on the planet."

Leo opened his mouth to refute the point, but he couldn't come up with an argument. "Okay, fine. But I always thought—I don't know, I dated a lot. I told myself I was looking for something. Not running away from it. But I think... I know, I see now, that the men I chose... it was never going to go anywhere between us. And that's how I wanted it."

"Boy, you really took the red pill, huh?" She hopped closer. "What prompted this introspection?"

Oh, just the startling realization that I'm falling for your witch. "I don't know. It's not any one thing, I guess." The way Cole smiled, or the kindness in his eyes, or his silly jokes. His selflessness. His perky nipples and round butt. "I don't want to be afraid anymore."

For a second Niamh didn't say anything. Then she flew over to the counter and retrieved Cole's ever-present magic bag, which she dropped in front of him. It skidded toward him on the table. "Go on," she encouraged. "Sounds like you need one."

Leo pulled out a lemon fizzy and popped it into his mouth, feeling better in spite of himself, and mustered his courage. "The thing is, I still can't do anything. Even if I wanted to—to try something different. I'm stuck. Cursed."

"No wonder you're in a mood." Niamh hop-flapped back to the counter. "Come on. Get these dishes into the dishwasher. Then you have a date with something silly on Netflix."

"I didn't know you had a degree in medicine," Leo joked flatly, but he got up and did what she said. Now that the words had come out, he felt too tired to wash anything by hand. The couch, a blanket, and some mindless entertainment sounded like the perfect balm.

He loaded the dishwasher for the second time, checked the doors, turned out most of the lights, used the bathroom. Then he dropped onto the couch. Niamh dragged his blanket over from the end and nudged the remote at him, and they watched bad heartfelt CBC dramas until Leo finally fell asleep.

Chapter Fourteen

LEO left the house Sunday afternoon with two lemon fizzies in his scrubs pocket, just in case. Even if they only had a mild effect, he didn't want to be under the influence of anything he didn't understand.

But if a—a werewolf showed up in the ER or something, well. Leo wanted to be prepared.

"Are you sure you don't want me to go with you?" Niamh had asked as he slipped into his shoes.

If he were honest, Leo did. But—"I have my cell phone if I need advice," he said. "And won't you be bored while I'm at work?"

"Bored!" Niamh crowed. "Hardly. Do you know how many people leave shiny wrappers on the ground outside hospitals?"

She was a magpie, after all.

But Leo left without her, telling himself he needed to do this alone to prove he could.

And he did.

Between taking patients' vitals, administering medications, checking IV lines, and all the recordkeeping that came with it, Leo didn't have time for flights of fancy about who might be lurking or which of his patients might belong to a world Leo had only just discovered.

"How's the nausea today?" he asked Mrs. Chifor, who had septicemia from a ruptured appendix. "Having any more luck keeping things down?"

"As long as I don't eat anything to begin with." She stared at him with flat, sunken eyes. "This is the most effective diet I've ever been on."

Leo didn't mistake that for a good thing. He nodded and started writing in her chart. "Well, the antibiotics you're on for the infection can cause nausea, and the sepsis doesn't help. I'll make a note for your doctor to consider a different antibiotic, or maybe lower your dosage if he thinks you're responding well enough. Meanwhile I can up your antiemetic. You want me to have them send up some applesauce? It's easy on the stomach." Too bad he didn't have any of Cole's mint candies to give her. A little magic wouldn't go amiss.

Mrs. Chifor gave an anemic shrug. "Why not."

If they didn't get her nausea under control soon, they'd have to put her on IV fluids. "How's the pain otherwise?"

"When I'm not throwing up? Four, maybe?"

"Better than yesterday, then. That's good." He finished his notations. "You need anything else?"

She didn't, so Leo left her to it and moved on to his next patient.

"Good weekend?" Jimmy asked him as they crossed paths at the fourth-floor nurses' station.

"Yeah, actually," Leo said, hoping he didn't sound as surprised as he felt. "A little unusual, but otherwise good. You?"

Jimmy lifted a shoulder. "I picked up an extra couple shifts. Car needs new tires. Winter is coming, blah blah blah." No wonder he looked tired.

"I'll make sure the coffeepot stays on."

"You're the best," Jimmy said around a yawn.

Leo grabbed five minutes for a coffee and a vending-machine chocolate bar—admittedly his preferred vice over candy—before getting back to work.

Afternoon faded into twilight, which dimmed into evening. Jimmy seemed to have traded tasks with someone and pulled desk duty, because he sat yawning at the nurses' station, a giant travel mug next to him. He looked up as Leo passed, blinked at him, then looked back at his screen. Then back at Leo.

"All right?" Leo asked.

Jimmy groaned and admitted, "I forgot what I was going to say."

By the time Leo was checking on Susan Andrews (tonsillectomy), night had fallen and the hospital was quiet. Susan wasn't alone, though. She never was.

"Hi, Susan. Hi, Dolly."

Susan lifted one weathered hand in a wave and mouthed *hello*. Dolly smiled, deepening the crease lines around her eyes. "You look tired, darling. How come they keep giving you the late shift?"

"Somebody's gotta do it." Leo smiled. "How are you doing today? You've got to be about ready to go home."

Yes, please, Susan mouthed.

Dolly raised Susan's other hand—she'd been holding it in her own—to her lips and kissed the back. "In good time."

In a different situation, tonsillectomies were essentially outpatient procedures. But between Susan's age and her heart condition, she'd been in the hospital for almost two weeks.

"Looks like the doctors think that could be as soon as tomorrow." Leo checked her monitors, temperature, pulse. "Pain still bad, I'm guessing."

Susan's flat stare spoke volumes.

He wondered if Cole had anything for that. "Adult tonsillectomies suck, I know."

"At least I can be here now," Dolly said, a bit misty-eyed. "If this had happened when we were younger… well, I doubt we could have sneaked under her mother's radar back then. Not if I was at the hospital all day and night."

Work, Susan reminded her, but her eyes were soft.

"It must have been hard for you both."

"Well, it wasn't easy." Dolly turned a soft, affectionate gaze on Susan. "But it was easier than being apart."

Leo's heart gave a definite pang as he made his notes. When he looked up again, Susan and Dolly were still staring at each other, still holding hands. Still so obviously in love. Leo had never dated anyone he'd want to visit him every day while he recovered from a tonsillectomy. "You're lucky to have each other."

Susan squeezed Dolly's hand and nodded.

"What about you, Leo?" Dolly asked. "You're a handsome fella. You must have someone waiting for you to come home tonight."

I hope so, Leo thought. Until Cole broke the curse, though, Leo wouldn't know for sure. "It's complicated."

"Oh, sweetheart." Dolly shook her head. "Life's too short for that."

Tell me about it. He finished his notes and set the chart down. "Everything's looking good. Any concerns?"

"Just how I'm going to stay awake on the drive home."

Well, that Leo could help with, at least. "Come with me and I'll get you a shot of caffeine sludge." He needed to go back to the nurses' station anyway.

When he got back to the station, Jimmy was nowhere to be found. Leo poured Dolly a paper cup of industrial-strength coffee.

"You're a lifesaver," Dolly proclaimed, cradling the cup. Then she smiled impishly. "Probably literally too, in your line of work. You have a quiet evening, you hear? You deserve it."

Leo repressed a horrified shudder. That had to be some kind of jinx. "Looking that way," he said as cheerfully as he could, and sent her on her way. The industrial lighting flickered over her head as she stabbed the button to call the elevator.

For a second Leo thought he saw something, a shadow in the stairwell at the end of the hallway.

But it must have just been a trick of the light. One of those night shift quirks. Leo put it out of his mind and went back to work. Less than an hour to go on his shift. Where the hell was Jimmy?

By now most of the patients were asleep. Leo checked the monitors, made his notations, and exchanged tired glances with Deborah, the orderly. "You see Jimmy anywhere?"

She shook her head. "Haven't seen him in an hour, maybe. Check the bathroom? That takeout he had in the fridge smelled questionable."

Ugh. Leo winced. "I'll check the bathroom." He hoped he wouldn't have to get Jimmy admitted. He'd never go home on time.

Back to Cole's on time, rather.

But the bathroom was empty, so that was a bust. Well, if Jimmy wanted to risk his job, that was his prerogative. The next shift was starting to come in, so Leo didn't feel at all guilty finishing his paperwork and preparing to leave.

Downstairs in the locker room, he grabbed a towel from the stack and opened his locker to get his flip-flops for a shower. He didn't want to wake Cole when he got home, and if he didn't shower before bed, he'd wake up smelling like hospital. He left his clean clothes in a pile on the bench, tossed his scrubs into the laundry bag, and toed on his shower shoes. Yawning, he hung his towel around his neck and stepped into the shower room. Steam already filled the room—Leo had never known this place to run out of hot water—and he breathed deeply, feeling the tension begin to release from his shoulders.

At least, until he saw the feet.

They were clothed, wearing the sort of comfortable, functional sneaker nurses preferred. Swallowing, Leo took a step closer. Scrub bottoms—had Jimmy been wearing blue? Leo couldn't remember. These were soaked through with warm water.

Leo pulled the towel from his neck and tucked it around his waist. He didn't think he wanted to be naked for whatever happened next.

Jimmy slumped against the wall under the spray of the water, his skin pink from the heat, except for his cheeks, which were pale. He was clothed, and his eyes were open, but he didn't answer right away when Leo called his name.

"Jimmy," Leo repeated, and finally Jimmy turned to look at him, blinking slowly.

Jesus.

"Come on," Leo said, reaching down. "Let's get you off the floor."

"I...." Jimmy looked down at his hands as though perplexed.

Leo followed his gaze. What the hell? "Jimmy, you decide to shower with two hundred bucks?"

He seemed to come back to himself. "That's my money. I found it."

"Uh-huh," Leo said. "You can keep it, come on. Get up."

He helped Jimmy back to the locker-room bench and grabbed him a towel. "I just couldn't get warm, you know?" Jimmy said as Leo wrapped him up. "I thought the hot water would help."

"Smart," Leo said, because hey, he'd been treating himself for shock. All that nursing training paid off. Sort of. "What made you so cold in the first place?"

Leo had his suspicions. And when he saw the two neat puncture wounds on the side of Jimmy's neck—no longer bleeding, because Roman, or whoever had bitten him, wasn't a complete asshole—that cemented it.

"Don't remember," Jimmy said, wiping water from his face. "Someone came to the nurses' station and we were talking. And then I couldn't get warm, so I came down here."

A vampire bite after what Leo reckoned as ten straight twelve-hour days. No wonder Jimmy had reacted poorly, especially if he hadn't known to eat and drink after. "I'm gonna go grab you a Gatorade." He hastily put his scrub pants back on. "Hang tight, okay?"

It took just a few minutes to get the Gatorade, and another five to get Jimmy to drink it while Leo monitored his vitals as surreptitiously as one could do to another nurse. Then Leo took the world's fastest shower and scrambled into his home clothes. "Hey, Jimmy. Can I drop you at home? I don't think you should be driving right now."

Jimmy nodded.

Getting organized to leave the hospital took longer than Leo would have liked, mostly on account of how slowly Jimmy moved getting into his dry clothes. Leo stopped at the McDonald's drive-through on the way to his place and ordered him a couple of cheeseburgers, which Jimmy inhaled as though he'd been fasting for a week. And then he got Jimmy inside, checked his vitals again, and recommended he call in sick tomorrow.

"'M off tomorrow," Jimmy murmured, so small mercies.

Leo let himself out of Jimmy's rented bungalow and stood on the concrete steps in the autumn chill, looking up at the moon. A hazy circle surrounded it. Leo's mom had once said that was a bad omen. He wondered if she knew she was right.

Roman had liked to go for walks with Leo after he got off shift. Leo couldn't see much outside the halo of a streetlamp, but Roman never had any trouble peering into the darkness—he'd navigated them around skunks and deer and, once, a coyote. And who knew how many other creatures of the night whose secrets he'd kept.

If Roman was watching now, Leo couldn't tell. But he wouldn't be cowed. "So you're stooping so low you're buying meals from exhausted nurses," he said, shoving his hand into his pocket. It closed around a lemon fizzy. "Maybe make sure it's not one who's been skipping meals and picking up extra shifts next time. You could've really hurt him."

Not the way he hurt Leo, though.

"And don't follow me, or I'll sic my witch on you," Leo added as he opened his car door. There. That should take care of it.

Unless, of course, the vampire who'd bitten Jimmy wasn't Roman at all. But he didn't think of that until he was snug on Cole's couch, Niamh trilling softly on her perch next to him, and as exhausted as he was, the thought didn't keep him awake.

"YOU were late last night."

Leo turned over on the couch and fell onto the floor.

Very late, apparently, Cole thought, taking the coffee out of the cupboard. He hadn't meant to wake him. "Sorry. Thought you were awake. Well, awake-er."

"S'okay." Leo sat up, shirtless—damn him—and with his hair in total disarray. It had grown enough now that it almost flopped into his eyes without product to keep it in place. "Didn't mean to wake you up when I got in. Weird night." He rubbed his eyes with the back of his hand. "Time's it?"

"Noon. Danielle's opening for me today. Everything all right?"

"Not really."

Cole paused in scooping out the coffee beans and turned to the living room. Leo had discarded the blanket and was standing in Cole's living room in his boxers, showing off his broad shoulders and defined chest. A fine trail of golden-blond hair led to things Cole couldn't afford to think about. And with bedhead and pillow creases on his face, Leo looked deliciously like he'd just rolled out of Cole's bed instead of off his couch.

"What happened?" Cole finally managed to convince his brain to say.

"Roman happened."

Cole's blood froze. "What? He came after you at work?"

Leo shook his head, padding into the kitchen. Cole didn't know that there was room enough for both of them when Leo was dressed like that. *Un*dressed like that. "Not for me. At least, I didn't see him. But someone bit my coworker. I found him in the shower after my shift, trying to get warm."

"Oh hell. What does he want?" Wasn't the curse enough revenge?

Unless Roman wasn't responsible for the curse at all. But then why—

"Blood, apparently." Leo lifted a shoulder and every single muscle in his body moved at one time, each clamoring for Cole's undivided attention. "He told me once hospitals were good places to grab a meal. Most of the staff aren't squeamish about blood. But Jimmy'd worked ten in a row and had a bad reaction."

"He was lucky he had you."

"Maybe. Or maybe, if it weren't for me, he wouldn't have been bitten at all."

Cole crossed his arms, about to take Leo to task for assigning himself blame he had no business taking, but then Leo continued.

"Then again, it's entirely possible he went into the whole thing with his eyes wide open. He did get two hundred bucks for his trouble."

Cole whistled. "Your ex must be flush."

With a shake of his head, Leo deadpanned, "Nah, he's about as pale as you'd imagine."

They exchanged grins over that, and their eyes met and held until Cole's whole body went pleasantly warm. But then it went on a beat too long, and he remembered he had a task here. "Coffee?"

Only he forgot to break eye contact, so he was still staring into Leo's fathomless baby blues when Leo said, "Please."

Cole's brain went to the bad place. He swallowed, paralyzed. Maybe he should avoid the kitchen if this kept happening. He was only human. One of these days he'd give in and....

And he didn't know what would happen then, so he turned and picked up the coffee beans. Grinding them gave him an excuse to turn his whole body away from Leo and get his heart rate under control.

Without the proximity of Leo's chest to distract him, reality came crashing back. "Is it safe for you to go to work? Maybe you should take a leave of absence."

Cole was reaching for the canister of the coffee grinder when something brushed against his arm. He looked over... and immediately regretted it. Because Leo was leaning back against the counter, stretching his lean, muscular body as though he were about to jump up and sit on the counter. The pose pulled his boxers tight across his front, almost as though he were inviting Cole to look.

Cole filled the canister and set it back on the grinder perhaps a little harder than necessary.

"Can't," Leo said. "The hospital's understaffed as it is. That's part of why I moved here. They need me. There's a reason Jimmy could pick up work ten days in a row."

Damn. Cole gritted his teeth and hit the button on the grinder to give himself a chance to think of something else. "Maybe Danielle can work some extra shifts this week. I could come with you."

"That would almost definitely violate hospital policy and my patients' privacy." Leo raised both arms over his head and went up on his tiptoes to stretch. A wave of warm air carrying hints of soap and sweat and skin wafted under Cole's nose. "But I appreciate the offer."

You're killing me, Cole thought. It took two tries to get the coffee canister off the grinder. He did better scooping the coffee into the french press, at least. How was he supposed to keep Leo safe without his cooperation?

"Anyway, Niamh already offered."

Cole corrected carefully before he could accidentally pour boiling water all over the counter. "She did?" he asked as he set the timer on the microwave.

"Night before last." Leo turned and stretched on his tiptoes to take some mugs from the cupboard—unnecessary; he was taller than Cole. And had better musculature in his back and ass. "I turned her down, but I might take her up on it after all." His arm brushed Cole's again as he set the mugs on the counter.

This time Cole couldn't make himself move away.

Would it be so bad? To find out once and for all if Leo was just *pushing* him, testing the boundaries of the curse, just *horny*, or if he might...? All Cole had to do was try to kiss him.

Try to kiss him, and hope the universe let him have just this one thing.

"Yeah, that's... not a bad idea." Cole gathered his strength and looked over. If he'd been winding Cole up on purpose, Leo gave nothing away now. "And you know you can always call me whenever if you need, like. Advice. Or a daring rescue."

Leo smiled. "Yeah, Cole. I know."

Cole's heart thundered. He was going to do it. His eyes locked with Leo's for a split second, and then Leo dropped his gaze to Cole's mouth, and Cole wasn't going to get a clearer signal than that. He licked his lips and took a breath—

Beep, beep, beep.

His coffee spoon would have made an unsatisfying projectile. Cole doubted it weighed enough to break the window, for example. So he set it on the counter and pushed down the plunger in the french press instead, using firm, steady pressure to strangle the caffeine out of the macerated beans.

Then, calmly, he poured two mugs of coffee, carefully keeping his eyes on his task. "Here," he said quietly, sliding the mug toward Leo without looking up.

For a second Leo didn't move, and Cole thought maybe he'd offended him, but then he took the mug. "Thanks," he said back, no louder than Cole.

It sounded like it hurt.

Chapter Fifteen

FRIDAY afternoon Cole left Leo to his own devices to make his standing date at Gran's. But instead of turning right out of his driveway, the most direct route, he found himself turning left, then left again. A minute later he parked opposite Peaseblossom and locked the car. He waved at Andre through the window of Caffeine and then jogged across the street.

Avery was standing on a ladder, retrieving some aluminum pots from a shelf above the register, when Cole walked in. "Cole," he said cheerfully, handing the pots down. "Do me a favor and take these?"

Cole grabbed them and set them on the counter while Avery climbed down.

"Thanks. Hey, how's your mundane? Did you find out who sent that vase?"

"Not yet." Cole glanced into the refrigerator. No daffodils this time, but he'd make it work. "But I will. I'm actually here as a paying customer."

"Oooh." Avery slung his leg over the barstool behind the counter and leaned forward, chin propped on his hands. "You gonna make an honest man of him?" he asked, fluttering his eyelashes.

Cole's ears burned with guilt. He *should* bring Leo flowers. He wondered if he could, if the curse would let him. He could probably pick up a bouquet and bring it home, anyway.

But he hadn't come here for that.

"I...."

Avery wrinkled his nose. "Read that wrong, huh?"

"No," Cole said. "Not exactly. Just... not yet. I want to get some flowers for my grandmother, actually."

"Well. You've come to the right place. Anything in particular?" Avery got off the stool and stood next to the refrigerator.

Cole looked at the flowers, considering. "Are those anemones?"

Avery gave him a sharp look. "Yeah."

"I'll take some of those," Cole said decisively. "And the white chrysanthemums."

Avery nodded and took out the flowers and a bucket of greenery to start an arrangement. "You want a couple of peonies in here too?" he asked, voice carefully neutral.

"That sounds nice," Cole agreed, confirming nothing.

A moment later Avery finished the arrangement, but the anemones drooped a little. Avery frowned at them. "Sorry, they're almost at the end of their life. Would've had to chuck them if they didn't go today. Here, just let me...." He caressed the stems and the flowers straightened, the blossoms tightening almost imperceptibly. He smiled. "It won't last, of course, so those are still half off."

Cole paid him and got back into the car.

Gran was waiting for him on the porch when he arrived, Gran was waiting for him on the porch, sitting in the swing and sipping from a mug of herbal tea. Cole trotted up the steps, bouquet in one hand, gumdrops in the other. "Gran," he said warmly, leaning down to peck her on the cheek. "I know, I know. I'm later than usual. But I brought you flowers!"

"Cole! They're lovely." Gran accepted the bouquet with a smile, but Cole watched carefully, and he saw the flash of recognition she tried to mask. "Let me go get a vase."

Cole followed her inside and took off his shoes, which he carried with him. "Do you need help with dinner?"

"Oh no, sweetheart. But if you wouldn't mind—"

Cole was already at the back door, putting his shoes on again. "What's on the docket this time?"

Without looking up from cutting the ends off the flowers, Gran answered, "Angelica, please. It's been done long enough now that it's gone to seed."

He wouldn't need the boline today, then; with angelica, they used the whole plant, roots included. "Spade in the garden shed?"

Gran nodded, and Cole went out the back door.

The garden shed had been built at the same time as the house, but it hadn't been maintained the same way. The door hinges were rusty, some of the wooden paneling had rotted, and Kate and Cole had accidentally broken one of the windows when they were children, and now only a thick plastic sheet covered the opening. But the bare light bulb still flickered on when Cole pulled the cord—after which he grimaced and wiped the cobwebs on his jeans—illuminating a grim, dusty graveyard of tools older than his mother.

He didn't see the spade right away. On the rickety shelf nailed to the wall were the bells the girls rang on Beltane. A filthy rake with a broken handle stood propped up against the remaining window.

Finally he found the spade; it had fallen onto its side on the floor and was hiding in the shadow of a derelict charcoal barbecue. But where was the cauldron? Gran had an ancient, rusty thing she used to keep out here for harvesting whole plants. More effective for retaining the plants' power than a plain old plastic bucket. But Cole couldn't find the cauldron, so the bucket it was.

Sometime when he hadn't been paying attention, the end of September had given way to mid-October, and the air held a definite chill as Cole dug the blade of the shovel into the ground around the angelica. The first half of the plants he put whole into the bucket, shaking as much dirt from the roots as he could. The second half he laid on the ground and beheaded with the shovel before sprinkling the seed pods back on the ground for next year.

Then he stashed the shovel in the shed and brought the angelica up to the porch so he could wash it in the laundry tub. "All done," he announced, toeing his shoes off outside the door. "Shall I hang them in the pantry?"

Gran looked up from peeling carrots. A roast, then—apparently she wanted to hold him hostage for a few hours. "No, downstairs, please, Cole. Angelica needs to dry a bit colder."

Cole took the plants into Gran's laundry room, just off the kitchen. After he cleaned them, he grabbed the roll of jute from above the laundry tub and turned to take the stairs down to the basement.

Sitting on top of Gran's chest freezer, scrubbed clean of garden dirt, sat Gran's cauldron, which had resided in the garden shed for as long as Cole could remember.

He bit his tongue and took the herbs down to dry.

"So," Gran said cheerfully as they finally sat down to dinner, "your latest client. Have you made any progress with him?"

Cole barely resisted the urge to grit his teeth. "Getting there," he answered, matching her tone. "I don't think it'll be much longer."

Gran nodded.

Cole mercilessly speared a carrot. "Do you think," he started, but he couldn't decide how to finish the sentence.

"Yes?" Gran prompted.

Fuck it. "Do you think I'll ever meet someone?"

Gran looked stricken.

"Because I would like that," Cole went on, horrified when his voice cracked like a teenager's. "I think I'm a good person. I try to help people. I recycle. Don't I deserve to be happy?"

"Cole—"

But now that he'd started, he couldn't stop. "I don't know what it is," he said. "But ever since I was a teenager, ever since the very first time I had feelings for someone—you always told me I had to listen to what the universe was telling me. That it has a way of keeping things in balance. Well, I've listened. But it's hard, Gran, and I need you to tell me: Am I supposed to be alone forever?"

Gran's face was ashen, and the skin around her eyes had gone tight. He hated upsetting her. But God. God, he was tired, and lonely, and he wanted so much more than he'd been allowed.

Cole set down his fork. He couldn't eat now anyway. "Julie got to find someone. And Aunt Hilda and Aunt June. Even Mom. I know you didn't like Geoff, everyone knows you didn't like Geoff, but—but the *universe* likes him. Likes them together." He took a shuddering breath. "Everyone is allowed to have someone—except me."

Gran's face crumpled. "Cole… sweetheart. I know it's lonely."

"I just want to know why. Why not me?" The question felt like it ripped out of his chest, leaving his heart exposed, and before he could stop it, his most carefully hidden fear tumbled out of the wound. "Is it because I'm gay?"

"No!" Gran burst out, tears in her eyes. "No, Cole, I promise you, the universe doesn't care about that."

Cole wanted to believe her. He did. But she always knew more than she let on, and he was tired of being told to accept scraps. "But you won't tell me anything else." She never did. He pushed back from the table. "I'm sorry, I can't… I can't stay for dinner tonight, Gran."

He made it to the car before his vision blurred completely, and he spent a miserable minute trying to staunch his tears on the sleeve of his T-shirt. But just as suddenly as the emotions had overwhelmed him, they fled again, leaving him clearheaded and determined. He couldn't live his life to please anyone but himself. And he wasn't going to live in fear anymore.

He hoped the universe would understand.

Chapter Sixteen

LEO was in the kitchen when Cole came in, determination burning bright within him. Niamh took one look at him and made her escape through the open kitchen window without so much as a by-your-leave, and Leo turned a curious look on Cole. He opened his mouth as though to ask a question, but Cole didn't give him the chance.

"Do you ever miss dancing?"

Leo blinked, and his mouth worked soundlessly for a moment, and his cheeks pinked. "I... yeah, I do."

"Good." Wait, maybe Cole's enthusiasm was getting away with him. He didn't want Leo to think he was happy Leo was miserable. "Come out with me tonight."

The lovely pink flush deepened and spread to Leo's ears and neck. "Tonight? I thought... don't you have dinners with your gran on Fridays?"

It was sweet that he remembered, but Cole didn't want to think about Gran right now. "Not this week." Despite Leo's lack of answer, his determination didn't wane. He didn't know what cards Kate would have read for him, and he didn't have her gift. But he was standing on the cusp of something tonight. They both were. "Come on," he said again. "What do you say?"

He didn't worry that the curse would prevent Leo from accepting. It had loosened enough; Cole could see it, could practically taste it. And when Leo ducked his head and smiled, quiet and almost bashful, before raising his head again and meeting Cole's eyes, Cole knew.

Leo said, "All right."

THROUGH some happy accident or miracle of foresight, Leo had actually picked up one of the polo shirts he typically wore clubbing when he'd swung by his apartment weeks ago. The thin material fit him like a second skin, and the color matched his eyes, not that most of his pickups would've noticed on the dance floor. When he put it on after a quick shower, his stomach tightened in anticipation.

Maybe tonight, finally. Cole had asked him to go dancing, and he'd said yes. Maybe the curse was breaking.

Cole must have been getting dressed in his bedroom, because he wasn't downstairs when Leo finished in the bathroom. Niamh was, though, flitting from chair back to chair back in the kitchen, squawking when she saw Leo. "Well. You clean up nice."

"Thanks." Leo fought the urge to fidget. "You wouldn't happen to know if this is… I mean. Would it be okay with you if I… if Cole…."

Niamh crowed a laugh. "Sweetheart, if I had any objections to you dating my witch, I'd have run you off long before now."

Leo flushed.

Before he could say anything, footsteps on the hardwood alerted him to Cole's presence, and he turned around. Cole had put on dark-wash jeans and a touchably soft green T-shirt that bore an avocado and the slogan Rock Out With Your Guac Out. The peaks of his nipples refused to play second banana to the ridiculous slogan, which would have been distracting enough on its own. Cole himself looked sheepish, though: he gave Leo a once-over, and his ears and neck went red, and he stuffed his hands in his back pockets. *Please don't draw more attention to your chest*, Leo thought wildly. "Wow," Cole said. "Maybe I should change."

Four months ago Leo might not have given Cole a second look. Now Leo needed him to understand Leo liked *this* version of him, with the silly T-shirts and the bad jokes and the heart of gold. "Don't you dare."

They both blushed until Niamh scolded them that their cab had arrived.

The town boasted exactly one gay bar, which reflected well on it, considering it didn't even have a Starbucks. Not much reflected well on the bar, however, largely because it was too dirty to reflect anything.

Cole paid the driver and their cover, and they went inside.

Zippers took advantage of the lack of competition to boast sticky floors, an ambiance that reeked of cheap beer and too much cologne, and the sort of plastic chairs Leo remembered from high school classrooms. At least that would make cleanup easier, he supposed, if cleanup was in fact a thing that occurred at Zippers.

But the bar took up one entire long wall, drinks cost half what they did in the city, and the DJ kept the dance floor packed with opportunities.

Leo loved this place.

"I'm gonna hit the bar," Cole said, leaning close so Leo could hear him over the throbbing bass. "You want something?"

Leo wanted something, all right, but Zippers didn't have it on tap. "Let me get it this time. Are you actually drinking?"

"I'll take their sweetest cocktail," Cole said, grinning.

Leo glanced around, but considering the volume, no one would overhear. "Not worried about mixing magic and booze?"

Someone bumped Cole from behind, knocking him into Leo's chest, but it didn't faze him. If anything, when he looked up at Leo with a hand between his pecs for balance, he positively smoldered. "Not tonight."

It took Leo a handful of heartbeats to remember that he was supposed to be doing something. "Sweet drinks," he said, turning toward the bar. "Coming right up."

Cole smiled and disappeared onto the dance floor.

Like the last few times he'd been here, Leo had the slight handicap of being unable to flirt with the bartender. Fortunately Tanya was an old friend, or as old as it got for Leo in these parts, and she didn't much appreciate male company anyway.

"Well, well, well. The cat came back."

"I just couldn't stay away." Leo dug his wallet out of his pocket. "I need your sweetest cocktail, please. And my usual."

Tanya raised an eyebrow as she snagged the grenadine. "Two drinks, huh? You back on the horse?"

Now there's a choice of words. "We'll see how tonight goes," he hedged, not wanting to jinx it, and slid a twenty across the bar. "Thanks, Tanya."

"Go get 'im, tiger."

Leo took the drinks and went to look for Cole.

It was early still, and the club was only at half capacity. Leo found Cole dancing in a small group near the edge of the dance floor and sidled up behind him.

"Brought you something," he said, leaning close to Cole's ear.

Cole tilted his head back, and suddenly their bodies pressed together from shoulder to hip. He smiled, slow and lazy, and took the drink—easy to spot, since Leo was drinking gin and tonic and Cole's was bright purple. The group fell away, and Cole swayed against Leo to the beat of the music vibrating through the sticky floorboards.

"Is it just like you remembered?" Cole asked, head still tilted so Leo could see his face.

He took a chance with the curse and moved his empty hand to Cole's hip. "No," he said honestly, then leaned the side of his face against Cole's so he wouldn't have to look when he added, "It's better."

Leo felt Cole smile against his cheek, and then he covered Leo's hand with his and moved it low over his stomach.

For a handful of heartbeats, the blood rushing in Leo's ears drowned out the beat of the music. All he could do was let Cole guide his body until the sense returned.

Even when it did, though, Leo followed Cole's lead. They finished their drinks and discarded the glasses on the nearest table. Then Cole pulled him deeper into the thickening crowd of writhing dancers.

Other bodies moved against Leo's now, but his attention never strayed from Cole: the heat of his body under Leo's hands, the scent of his witchy soap and clean sweat, the sweet confidence with which he *looked* at Leo, inviting him closer. The sweep of his eyelashes. The red-purple stain of his mouth.

The beat changed and Cole turned, slotting one of his thighs between Leo's and draping his arms around Leo's neck. Leo slid his hands into Cole's back pockets, peripherally appreciating the firm, round curves, but Cole's eyes held him captive now, full of desire and promise. Leo thought the curse must be broken. The curse was broken and he'd fallen under a new enchantment, only this time magic had nothing to do with it.

Leo leaned down so their foreheads touched, and Cole drew him closer still. Another breath and their lips would brush. Leo held his breath in anticipation. Any moment now—

"Leo? Is that you? Holy shit, it is!"

Damn it.

Cole gave him a forgiving look as Leo raised his head. "Eric. Anton. Long time no see."

Cole slid his hands down Leo's arms, squeezed his hands, and excused himself to the restroom.

"I thought you didn't like us anymore," Eric said, looking pointedly after Cole. "But I see that's not the case."

"You've just found someone else you like better," Anton finished shrewdly. "No wonder we haven't seen you here. I bet he never lets you leave the house!"

Leo opened his mouth, ready to defend Cole, who wasn't the jealous type, but Eric snorted.

"He never lets *Leo* leave?" he scoffed. "I saw how they were looking at each other. If they never leave the house, it's because they can't keep their pants on long enough. He looked like he wanted to devour you right there on the dance floor."

I wanted him to. Leo gave them a strained smile and didn't bother correcting their assumptions. "It's good to see you guys. Maybe I can introduce you to Cole later?"

Anton and Eric exchanged glances. "Later?"

Leo couldn't possibly get any warmer than he'd felt pressed against Cole on the dance floor, but he managed to flush anyway. "I don't think we're going to be sticking around much longer."

Eric hooted with laughter, but Anton simply indicated over Leo's shoulder; Cole had just emerged from the restroom. "Good for you," he said, grinning as he shoved Eric into the writhing crowd. "Maybe we'll see you around."

LEO'S friends had gone by the time Cole returned from the bathroom. Excellent. Not that Cole would've minded meeting them, under different circumstances. But tonight he had other plans.

"Hey," Leo said as Cole got closer, encircling his waist with both arms. His body was firm under Cole's touch, but his eyes, his voice, the curve of his mouth were so, so soft.

Cole couldn't wait anymore. "Shut up," he murmured, raising his hands to Leo's face. His skin was soft too, under Cole's palms; he must have shaved after his shower. Leo didn't move, barely breathed except to lower his eyelids.

Cole closed his too and kissed him.

At the first touch of their lips something fell into place. Leo tightened his hands on Cole's waist and opened his mouth with a sound Cole couldn't hear over the music in the club but *felt* down to his toes. A heartbeat later Cole traced his tongue over Leo's bottom lip and into his mouth and moved his hands back, threading them into Leo's hair, a tangle of warm, fine silk.

The lines of the curse flared green, the frayed length of it tightening, brittle. And then Leo sighed against him and it disintegrated and Cole felt that too, tilting his head deeper into the kiss as Leo slid his hands down his back.

When the kiss broke, Leo was watching him with wide, hungry eyes. "Cole."

He shivered as the word went through him. "Let's go home."

It was early enough they didn't have trouble getting a cab. But they didn't touch in the back seat apart from the fervent clench of their hands together on the cracking vinyl. The car had barely stopped outside Cole's house when Leo passed the driver a twenty and pulled Cole out after him.

They kissed when the front door closed behind them, with Leo the aggressor and Cole happily plastered against the wood. They kissed on the stairs to the bedroom, knocking pictures askew as they tore at each other's clothes. At the landing, Cole's jeans tangled around his feet and he stumbled to his knees, and he and Leo dissolved into giggles. If the universe was trying to keep them apart, it would have to do better than that.

"Should've taken our shoes off downstairs," Leo said, bending to try to undo his laces but hobbled by his own denim. "This is bad house-manners karma."

Meanwhile Cole, kneeling, had worked his feet free and kicked his jeans off. "I forgive you," he said, swatting Leo's hands away from his shoes. Cole could do it faster—he dug his fingers into the laces and tugged until they loosened, Leo balancing with his hands on Cole's shoulders. He toed off his shoes and Cole looked up, questioning.

When Leo nodded, Cole curled his hands into Leo's waistband and pulled his jeans down.

That left Leo standing in formfitting black boxer briefs, his cock straining at the fabric. For a moment Cole forgot himself and stared, taking in the fine red-gold hair that led down from Leo's navel and clung to the tops of his thighs. Cole cupped the backs of Leo's ankles, intending to run his hands up slowly, take his time—but Leo slid his hands into Cole's hair instead and pulled him to his feet.

"You're killing me," he murmured, shoving Cole toward the bed. "I need to touch you too."

Cole landed on his back on the bed, legs splayed. "That seems fair," he agreed, reaching out his arms in invitation. "Where do you want to start?"

Only, instead of jumping on the bed like Cole expected, Leo stood rooted to the spot, expression nakedly hungry yet somehow apprehensive. What was going on in his head? "Leo?"

But the moment broke, and Leo shook his head. "I have no idea," he admitted quietly.

Oh. Well, Cole could help with that. "I have a couple ideas if you're open to suggestions." He waggled his eyebrows and patted the bed beside him. "But you're going to have to come a little closer first."

Leo climbed onto the other side of the bed. Before he could overthink it further, Cole kissed him, curling his body into Leo's so that their knees brushed, cupping the side of his face. Leo hummed into the kiss and the tension melted out of him, his hand going to Cole's waist, then his hip. Cole trailed his fingertips down Leo's throat to his chest, chasing goose bumps. He could have gotten lost in the valley between Leo's pectorals. Leo had better muscle definition than Cole, but also better than anyone Cole had ever met. With anyone else he might have been self-conscious, but he already knew how Leo felt about him, so self-consciousness seemed self-defeating. Leo correctly thought Cole was awesome.

And Cole was going to prove it, hopefully with sex.

"See," he gasped as Leo slid his hand under the waistband of Cole's boxers. "You didn't need my help after all."

Leo laughed through his nose, then shifted his weight and pulled until Cole was lying on top of him, braced over his shoulders, their groins aligned so Cole could feel Leo's dick hard next to his own. "I might need a *little* help," he said, both hands on the bare skin of Cole's ass now. Cole groaned, grinding down. "Don't think I can get these off without your cooperation."

"Oh, I'll cooperate in getting off." Cole planted his elbows on the bed and rose to all fours. "Don't worry about that."

This time Leo's laugh turned into a moan as Cole sucked kisses down his jawline toward his neck. "Oh, so now you're putting words in my mouth."

Cole grinned against his clavicle, then bit lightly, testing. Well, Leo had dated a vampire; it was an educated guess. Leo shivered pleasantly. "Really. You're gonna give me an opening like that?"

"That's not the only opening I'll give you," Leo promised, only it turned into a yelp when Cole bit his nipple, almost accidentally, in surprise at the blatant invitation. "God, do that again."

"Sorry, busy now," Cole murmured against his sternum, mouthing his way south. He slid his hands down Leo's chest to pluck at his nipples, though; he wasn't *heartless*. Another day he'd take his time and explore properly. But tonight—well, they'd waited long enough.

Leo's stomach twitched under Cole's lips when Cole reached his navel, and he nipped instead, then sat back to run his hands up Leo's thighs. "Hey, question: Should I use a condom to suck your dick?"

Leo groaned and his hips jerked under Cole's hands. "I work in a hospital. I had a panel done last week. All negative. The paper's in my jeans pocket if you want."

"Presumptuous!" Cole exclaimed, delighted. Those boxer briefs had taunted him long enough.

"Hopeful," Leo corrected, lifting his hips so Cole could finally, *finally* clap eyes and hands and mouth on all of him. Leo's dick was as beautiful as the rest of him, thick and hard, wet at the tip. "It's been a long *time*—"

He cut off on a high-pitched syllable as Cole took him in his mouth. He tasted as good as he looked, and he held completely still as Cole devoured him, pushing himself as far as he could go, until the head of Leo's cock bumped the back of his throat. Then farther.

"Oh God," Leo groaned, his thighs splaying open.

Cole ran his hands up the insides of his legs, caressing, and Leo opened more. Damn it, he should've grabbed the lube. He pulled back, licking his lips, teasing his thumbs along the crease of Leo's groin. "Can you reach the drawer?"

Leo's chest hitched with his breath as he reached over his head and slid the drawer open. He pulled out a brand-new bottle of lube and an unopened box of condoms. "Guess I'm not the only one who was presumptuous."

"Hopeful," Cole teased, biting lightly at the inside of Leo's thigh as Leo dropped the lube near his hip. "Maybe determined."

"Horny," Leo said as Cole put his lips back on his dick, reaching for the lube.

"Now who's putting words in whose mouth?" Cole murmured against the base of Leo's shaft.

Leo threaded his fingers into Cole's hair. "Trust me, words are not what I want to put in your mouth."

Cole licked the head of his cock, slow and showy. "What's stopping you?"

Nothing, now: he pushed Cole's head down. Cole went, humming in satisfaction, keeping his mouth just slightly too soft to satisfy. He trailed his left hand over Leo's thigh, cradled his balls. With his right, he opened the lube—thoughtfully unsealed before they'd left the house—and wet his fingers.

Leo's dick leaked steadily, his hand a welcome weight on the back of Cole's neck. And when Cole teased a finger between his cheeks and slid it across his hole, he made a keening sound Cole would be jerking off to for the rest of his life. His own cock throbbed in sympathy.

Leo let go of Cole's hair when Cole slid a finger inside him, instead fisting his hands in Cole's sheets, his biceps straining, legs flexing. Cole let his cock fall from his lips so he could concentrate on the whole of him, splayed out as a feast for Cole's senses: Cole could have devoured him with his eyes, or his hands, or his mouth, but the soft whines spilling from Leo's lips were just as delicious, and he smelled—sweet but earthy, like a garden in a rainstorm.

"Cole," Leo moaned, and Cole suddenly realized he had three fingers curled against Leo's prostate and had been massaging it, wringing out each beautiful sound. "Are you going to fuck me sometime this year? Because it has been a *long* four months, and I don't know if I can last four more."

Right. Cole carefully withdrew his fingers, relishing the quiet shudder of Leo's body. He pressed a kiss to the inside of Leo's thigh and lifted his head to search for the condoms, only to find Leo had one waiting.

"So it's like that," Cole said, but when he reached out to take it, Leo bent his knee and nudged Cole closer so he could do it himself. The first touch of Leo's hand on him had him biting his lip to hold in a gasp; Leo's grip was warm and knowing and firm. He stroked Cole root to tip, root to tip, then smeared the fluid at the head before rolling the condom down his length.

Leo arched an eyebrow. "No smartass remarks now?"

"Gnnh," Cole agreed. "On your back?"

Leo nodded frantically, and Cole grabbed the pillow from his side of the bed and shoved it under Leo's raised hips. "Good?"

"Could be better," he said breathily, and wrapped his leg around Cole's hip, digging his heel into his ass.

Cole didn't—couldn't—argue. He knee-walked closer, leaned down, braced himself on one arm. And then he pushed in.

Heat overcame him, bleeding from his cock to his balls to the small of his back, settling in his gut. Cole squeezed his eyes shut, struggling for control. Leo's body held him just right, from the clench of his ass to the cradle of his thighs to the hands that had come up to card through his hair again, and Leo arced into him, straining for more, and any tenuous grasp of self-possession Cole might have had fled.

He snapped his hips, lowering his head until their faces touched. Right away Leo tilted his head back so his breath filled Cole's ear, and Cole shivered. His hips snapped again of their own accord, drawing a punched-out cry from Leo. Then Leo pulled Cole's mouth to his in a wet kiss that made the hair on the back of Cole's neck stand up.

"Yeah," Leo murmured into Cole's mouth, the whisper lingering on Cole's skin. He cupped the hinge of Cole's jaw, thumb brushing Cole's ear.

Yeah, Cole agreed, and fell apart, thrusting wildly as Leo cried out beneath him, sliding his other hand down to dig his nails into the flesh over Cole's hips.

"Yeah," Leo said again, raising his hips to meet Cole, urging him on. Cole couldn't lift his head, too overcome, but he shifted his weight to his left arm and slid his right between them, encircling Leo's cock. "Cole—Cole, *fuck*," and wetness spilled over Cole's fist, and Leo clenched, and his nails dug into Cole's back *hard*, and Cole came, biting his lip to keep his words from spilling out.

When he could breathe enough to move without fainting, Cole pulled out and rolled carefully onto his side, keeping his legs close to Leo's, not wanting to lose the contact.

Leo let go of Cole's waist, but not his face, just holding him as they breathed in the intimate quiet. Their noses touched. Cole *ached* with it, with how much he felt for Leo and how much Leo must feel for him. He had wanted this his whole life; having it felt almost unreal.

Leo kissed him again, slow, without agenda. Cole melted into it, wondering at the etiquette: Was it rude to try to pull Leo closer when his available hand was covered in… Leo?

It turned out he didn't have to decide; a second later Leo shivered, and not in the pleasant way, and drew away from the kiss. "I would love to stay like this all night, but, uh, this is getting cold." He gestured.

"You look like a really muscular overfrosted donut," Cole observed before he could stop himself.

"Well, there's something I'll never eat again." Leo made a teasing face. "Let me go clean up."

Cole wanted to tell him no, to keep him in his bed and get a washcloth and a towel for him, but realistically, no washcloth was going to cut it. On impulse, he kissed Leo's nose. "All right, but hurry back."

The shower started in the bathroom, and Cole took a few seconds to clean himself up too. He was debating changing the sheets when the water turned off again and Leo appeared in the doorway.

"C'mere," Cole said, sliding into bed and patting the sheet beside him.

Leo obeyed, and Cole pulled up the blankets before turning out the light and curling his body toward Leo.

"This isn't going to be awkward tomorrow, is it?" Leo asked quietly after a moment, and Cole realized his advantage. He knew what would break the curse, and he knew what had broken it.

"Are you going to sneak out of bed and pretend this never happened?"

"No."

"Regret getting involved with another obscure and avoid me in the morning?"

"No."

"Steal my candy stash and run off with Niamh in the middle of the night?"

Leo snickered. "No."

Cole curled up a little. "Deny my need for postsex cuddling and break my heart?"

The sheets rustled and the bed dipped as Leo wormed closer, until he was close enough to coax Cole to turn onto his other side. Then he spooned up behind him, linked his hand with Cole's, and settled both over Cole's sternum. "Definitely not."

Something in Cole's chest loosened, and he closed his eyes, content. "Then I think we'll manage fine."

He fell asleep feeling Leo smile into his ear.

Chapter Seventeen

THE next few days might technically have exceeded the textbook definition of *managing fine*. For thirty-six hours they could barely keep their hands off each other, save for necessary breaks to eat and breathe. Monday and Tuesday were a variation on the theme, with work thrown into the mix. Reality reasserted itself Wednesday, though, when Leo left his towel on the bathroom floor and heard Cole cursing through the walls as he dressed for work.

"Sorry!" he half shouted back, only to turn around and find Cole holding the offending item, not quite managing a full glower. "I'll do better," he promised.

Cole shook his head and the rest of his scowl turned contemplative. "You really hate laundry, huh?"

"Uh… yeah." They'd never talked about it, but it must be obvious to someone he lived with—someone whose closet space he'd been borrowing for weeks.

"I'll make you a deal. I'll do laundry"—Leo debated getting on his knees and blowing him right then and there—"if you keep feeding me on a regular basis." Cole shrugged. "Cooking's too much like work to do it every day."

"Deal," Leo agreed immediately.

Cole shoved the damp towel into his arms and kissed his cheek. "Just make sure you get what's dirty in the laundry basket next time."

All things told, that seemed more than fair.

SATURDAY morning Leo woke up very late with Cole starfished on top of him and a bladder that demanded to be emptied. Still, he lazed in bed, reveling in a comfort he'd never take for granted again and a giddy, bubbly sensation in his chest. His body's satisfied aches reminded him the curse was thoroughly broken and had been for a week, but he contemplated waking Cole up to double-check anyway, just to be thorough. Eventually his bladder prevailed and he slipped out of bed to use the bathroom.

He must've woken Cole up, because the bed was empty when he returned. He borrowed a pair of shorts and a T-shirt from Cole's closet, concerned the downstairs curtains might be open, and found Cole in the kitchen, making hopeful eyes at the kettle. When he heard Leo, he turned around; his eyes were still half-closed and his hair was flat on one side and he was very warm against Leo's chest, which he snuggled into immediately.

"Hi," Leo said, folding his arms around him.

"Hi," Cole said into Leo's shoulder. After a deep breath he looked up, smiling, and touched the olives between Leo's pecs. "Nice shirt."

Leo grinned, the tips of his ears burning. "Thanks. I thought it was appropriate."

Cole went pink too and leaned their foreheads together. Then the kettle finished boiling and he made grabby hands at the coffee canister. "You want?"

"Please," Leo said, only half referring to the caffeine. "Breakfast?"

"Pancakes?"

"Sure." The fridge still harbored a handful of strawberries on the verge of furriness; he could slice those and sugar them as a fancier alternative to syrup. He opened the fridge and took out milk, berries, butter, eggs. Cole didn't bake much as far as Leo could tell, but he was pretty sure he'd seen some flour in the pantry, sandwiched between the enormous bags of sugar.

Something in the kitchen buzzed. "Is that your cell?" he asked, sticking his head into the pantry. There—flour, baking powder, salt. He juggled them in his arms and looked over his shoulder at Cole.

"Yeah. Nothing important." Cole slipped his phone into the pocket of his sweatpants. "Just a reminder."

A reminder about what? Leo set the ingredients on the counter and took a bowl out of a drawer. He was reaching for an egg when Niamh squawked, "Your cell phone's ringing," and he just about jumped out of his skin.

Clutching his chest, Leo stumbled back a step. "Jeez, Niamh. Can we get you a bell or something?"

Niamh alit on the back of a kitchen chair. "Sorry. But your phone is ringing. At least, I assume the phone in the jeans in the hallway is yours."

Leo was not going to let a talking bird make him blush again, neither at the reminder that he wasn't supposed to leave his clothes on the floor nor the fact that he and Cole kept tearing each other's clothes off. He did need to answer his phone, though. But he'd only taken two steps out of the kitchen when Cole said, "Leo?"

He stopped and turned, and Cole tapped his fingers against the small print underneath the olive motif, his eyes soft but sparkling. "Olive you too."

The kiss was still tingling against Leo's lips when he retrieved his phone—down to 10 percent battery life—and checked his messages.

Liz from the hospital, asking him to call back. Leo hit the contact and tucked the phone between his ear and shoulder.

Normally it took a few minutes to get through, but today Liz picked up on the second ring, sounding frazzled. "Leo, thank God. I know it's your day off, but Marco has the flu and Fiona just called in—she got in a car accident and thinks her leg's broken. I haven't been able to get ahold of Jimmy. Jess is on vacation in Florida. Is there any chance you can come in for a shift? Eight hours, double overtime."

Leo looked at the inviting mess of Cole's bed, the telltale scatter of clothes over the floor. He could hear Cole singing off-key as he made coffee. Autumn sunshine streamed in the windows, suffusing the bedroom with warmth. He desperately wanted to tell Cole to put the coffee away and drag him back up here to shut out the world for as long as they could. "There's no one else you can call?"

"Help me, Obi-Wan Kenobi. You're my only hope."

Leo closed his eyes and allowed himself one heartbeat of self-pity. Then he started looking for clean pants.

When he returned downstairs, Cole took one look at him—clothed—and put one of the mugs back in the cupboard. He took down a travel mug instead. "Duty calls?" he said a little forlornly.

"Even with me there, they're going to be shorthanded." Leo put his hands on Cole's waist and drew him in for a short kiss. "I'll make it up to you later?"

Cole pretended to consider it. "Hmm." Then he tilted his head back in a wordless demand for another kiss. Leo could get used to that—had already gotten used to it, it seemed, since he obliged without thinking. "Okay. I'll start brainstorming."

Leo laughed. "Sounds good."

Cole took a half step back and shoved his hands in his pajama pockets. "But take Niamh with you again." Leo had done that the whole previous week, because— "The curse might be broken, but we still don't know what Roman's plan was or why he was at the hospital the other day. He might try something else if he finds out his first plan didn't work."

"'Take Niamh with you,' he says." Leo looked at her. "Like you weren't even there. Rude. Niamh, could I impose? I'll buy you something shiny."

Niamh cocked her head. "I want a whole bag of Christmas tinsel."

"It's October!" Cole protested.

Whatever, Leo could definitely buy that on Amazon. "Done!" he said. "Let's go."

With the labor shortage, Leo hardly had time to think about Roman, the curse, or Niamh flitting from window to window as he worked. By seven, just an hour from the end of his shift, he started to think Cole had worried for nothing.

So of course that was when everything went sideways.

The sun slipped below the horizon as Leo was checking the vitals on a post-op patient. He shivered but figured it was just a random misfiring of his nervous system.

Then something tapped frantically on the window, and he just about dropped the patient's chart. When he had his limbs under control, he put the chart down and cranked open the window the few inches hospital regulations allowed.

"What?" he hissed, grateful for the anesthesia that meant his patient wouldn't be waking up anytime soon.

"Something's happening," Niamh whispered, hopping nervously from foot to foot. "At the ER drop-off." She jerked her head.

Leo followed her gaze to a familiar shiny black sports car and the bottom fell out of his stomach. "That's Roman's car."

"Find a long-term patient's room," Niamh advised, her movements quicker now, obviously agitated. "If they don't invite him in, you might be protected—"

But then Roman got out of the car and went to the back seat, where a familiar face leaned against the window, and Leo did something very stupid.

He booked it for the stairs.

His tennis shoes squeaked on the floor as he rounded the corner from the patient's room into the hallway, and he narrowly avoided colliding with an orderly. But then he had a straight shot to the stairwell, where he took the steps three at a time, his heart beating a thousand times a minute, his palms sweating. He hoped against hope as he burst into the ER waiting room just in time to see Roman set the body on the sidewalk outside the hospital. He met Leo's eyes, and for a bizarre second Leo thought he looked *regretful* as he melted into the shadows.

But Leo didn't have time to analyze Roman's motives. "Get me a gurney!" he shouted. He hit the door at full speed and dropped to his knees on the pavement, praying he'd find a pulse.

Jimmy's skin was cool and clammy, his eyes closed. Leo touched his wrist, not daring yet to check his neck, and leaned down. Had Roman waited too long? Had Jimmy—?

"Ready?" someone asked, and Leo realized the team he'd called for had arrived. On autopilot, he helped get Jimmy loaded onto the stretcher, and then one of the ER doctors took over.

"Slow pulse, shallow respiration. Patient seems to be in hypovolemic shock. Start an IV to push fluids and get him started on a transfusion. And get him a CT scan, we need to find out if he's bleeding internally. Go."

Leo went with the team, doing his best to keep calm, to keep Jimmy alive. If anyone was upset that he'd left his floor to help, they didn't mention it to him.

His shift went late. By the time Jimmy was stable and the transfusion was done—and a police guard posted, since he seemed to have been attacked—Leo's eyes were gritty and he was exhausted. He stood under the hot stream in the shower for five minutes, trying to wash away the sight of the neat puncture wounds on Jimmy's neck and elbow.

And then he remembered Niamh.

Shit.

He dried and dressed quickly, hopping without grace into his shoes. She was probably frantic; she'd told him to try to hide—

Cole was in the hospital waiting room, ashen-faced, gripping his phone so tightly his fingers were white. A crushing wave of relief washed over Leo as Cole stood, expression pinched. Before he knew it, Leo was throwing his arms around him, sinking into Cole's embrace as Cole curled his fingers in the back of his shirt.

"You asshole," Cole muttered into Leo's shoulder. "Niamh flew home and told me. I was fucking frantic. No one would tell me anything."

"Sorry," Leo said against the side of his head. "Sorry, sorry, I was with the doctors getting him stabilized, I went into emergency nurse mode. I didn't think about you and Niamh."

"She says you owe her two bags of tinsel now."

Leo shuddered in his arms, not caring who saw. People hugged in ER waiting rooms all the time. No one would begrudge him this. "I will buy her a damn case."

They stood like that until Leo could bear to let go a little, but even then Cole only pulled back far enough to look Leo in the eye. "How is he? Jimmy, right?"

"Hypovolemic shock," Leo said grimly. "He lost a lot of blood, but we think he got here in time to avoid organ failure." He raised a hand to his face to rub his eyes and realized he was shaking. His eyes stung. "Shit."

"I think I better drive you home." Cole put an arm around his shoulders and turned him toward the door. Leo leaned into his warmth, surprised when Cole took his weight without bending. "Come on. Did you eat?"

Leo tried to think. He'd had an energy bar or something a couple of hours before his shift was supposed to end. He didn't know how long ago that had been. "Not really."

"Soup," Cole said decisively. Then, "Oh." He reached his left hand into his jacket pocket and pulled out the ever-present candy bag. "Have one of the red ones."

He should have known Cole would medicate him with candy. Leo took one and popped it into his mouth, expecting peppermint. Instead it tasted of spiced apple cider, notes of cinnamon and maybe nutmeg and clove. It made him *feel* warm too, like he was snuggling under a blanket on the couch rather than being escorted out of the hospital. It was a simple thing, but it made his throat tight. "Thank you."

On the way home Cole stopped at a drive-through Tim Hortons for soup and steeped tea and, after a sideways glance at Leo, a chocolate-glazed donut.

"Do you think…," Leo started when they were home, seated at the kitchen table. He'd changed into a pair of Cole's too-small sweats, mainly for the comfort of wearing Cole's clothes.

Across from him, Cole met his eyes steadily, nudged his foot under the table. "What?"

Leo dropped his gaze to his soup, unsure how to phrase his question. He didn't want to make excuses for Roman. He was long past that. But something didn't add up. "I saw Roman drop Jimmy at the ER. But what I don't get is why. I mean, unless vampires can develop drinking problems, I guess. Is that a thing?"

"I don't know enough vampires to say, but I imagine if it's in human nature to do things to excess when you're mortal, that doesn't just go away when you give up sunlight and vegetables." Cole frowned. "Obviously he wasn't like that when you were dating?"

"No! He said he only needed to drink a few mouthfuls every week. There's no way he would've needed to do that to Jimmy. Certainly not twice," Leo said, warming to his subject. "And if he was going to turn into the kind of vampire who takes too much and leaves his victims barely clinging to life, why take him to a hospital and risk getting caught?"

"Huh." Cole considered that, toying with his paper cup. He'd finished his tea already by virtue of the fact that he'd ordered it with enough cream to make it tepid. "I don't know. And this wasn't your regular shift—it's not like he knew you were working, right?"

"Not unless he's got the hospital phone lines tapped or something."

"So presumably this wasn't some weird scare tactic."

"Yeah. But what, then?" Leo shook his head. "I mean, wounded pride is one thing. The curse was well designed, but the idea of it seems sort of... impulsive. And it didn't actually hurt anyone, blue balls notwithstanding."

Cole snorted. "A reputable source tells me those aren't a medical issue."

Leo blinked innocently. "So you're saying I don't need further treatment?"

"Well," Cole backpedaled. "I mean, an ounce of prevention, right? Just because there's no evidence to say—"

Leo nudged his foot under the table, and he shut up. "What I'm saying is, either he's escalating into very dangerous territory, or we're dealing with something else entirely."

Cole sighed. "Now there's a cheerful thought." Then he stood and went to the pantry, removing items seemingly at random and setting them on the counter.

Flummoxed—surely Cole wasn't hungry; he'd presumably had a regular dinner and he'd also eaten half Leo's donut—Leo said, "What are you doing?"

"Protection spell," Cole said grimly. "I have one on the house already, but another layer can't hurt. And you need an amulet. I should've made one weeks ago."

Leo watched in fascination, wondering what ingredients Cole had set out—whether he had these things on hand all the time or had bought them special. "I thought you said you don't have an active power." He'd had to have Kate charm his EpiPen to stay the right temperature, since he kept leaving it in the car. Leo had given him a hard time about that, but Cole was stubborn.

"I don't." Cole rummaged in a cupboard and pulled out a beat-up round-bottomed metal—a cauldron. He pulled out a cauldron. Just casually, from a cupboard where you'd keep any other pot. Leo wondered how he'd missed it before. "But any witch can cast a basic protection spell if they know the ingredients. Not much talent involved."

Cole poured ingredients into the cauldron, working by feel rather than with any measurement system Leo could see. "So how is this spell different from the one you already have?" If he was going to be caught up in this world, he might as well learn as much as he could about it.

"The existing one's more of a… warning?" Cole picked up something that, when he tipped it over, smelled like sulfur. "The broom by the front door is a low-level charm against mischief—always bristles up, otherwise it's unlucky." Something in the cauldron made a *whoomph* noise, and a little smoke rose. It was purple. "Mostly it lets other obscures know a witch lives here and they shouldn't mess with them."

Leo cocked his head. "But couldn't that also invite trouble? What if someone didn't like witches or wanted to use your powers for evil?"

"Use my powers for evil? Really?" Cole rolled his eyes. "You have a dimmer view of humanity—mundane and obscure—than I do." He uncorked a vial of something and the cauldron made a bubbling noise, despite the fact that Cole hadn't actually added anything to it. He put the cork back in. "Anyway, there's a protection spell around the house that'll make a hell of a noise if anyone comes here with ill intentions. It won't do much but wake me up—well, me and the rest of the neighborhood. And the exterior lights will come on."

"I suppose that would scare off most ne'er-do-wells."

Cole snorted, a smile playing at the corners of his lips. "You sound like my grandmother." Then he sobered and tossed a bunch of dried lavender into the pot, stems and all. "This one will go farther—it will actually repel those who come with malice in their hearts." He looked up and lifted a shoulder. "Sorry, I sound like a textbook."

"No, no, I'm enjoying the lesson." And watching Cole work helped take his mind off less pleasant things. He imagined watching Cole make candy would have much the same effect. "How come you haven't cast this before now?"

"Hasn't been a need." Cole finished off whatever he was doing with a handful of down feathers, then started putting the ingredients back in the pantry. Leo supposed he was lucky he hadn't accidentally put eye of newt in the artichoke dip the other night. "Besides, this isn't exactly going to be pleasant."

Before Leo could ask what he meant, he took a knife from the block on the island, closed the fingers of his left hand around it, and sliced.

"What are you *doing*?" Leo jumped out of his seat, the chair skittering across the floor as he reached for Cole's hand.

Cole dropped the knife and warded him off with his right hand, holding his left over the cauldron and squeezing, his face pinched. "I told you, it's not pleasant, but it's a necessary evil. So to speak." The mixture in the cauldron had turned to some kind of gray dust, with no trace of any of the individual ingredients.

"Will you at least let me clean it?" Cole had cut himself deeply. "I want to make sure it heals properly."

"When I'm done," Cole said. "Meanwhile, can you grab the lantern by the back door and light it? I'll need you to hold it as we walk the perimeter of the house. We could use a flashlight, but…."

"But?" Leo prompted.

Cole lifted the cauldron in his uninjured hand. "But you're totally geeking out about this, so why not go whole hog? Besides, I think I'm out of D batteries."

So Leo dutifully lit the lantern, holding it aloft so Cole could see what he was doing as he reached into the cauldron with his bleeding hand and spread the ash in an unbroken circle around the house. Somehow, despite the wind and everything Leo had ever observed about dustlike substances, the line remained solid.

"Almost done," Cole murmured, seemingly to himself. As the line he was spreading connected with the other end at the back door, it glowed briefly before disappearing.

Then Cole said, "Oh, wow. Yep. That was dumb," and wobbled a little on his feet.

Leo put an arm around his waist and helped him to a seat on the back porch bench. "I take it this is why you don't do this often."

Cole leaned against the trellis. "This wouldn't happen if I had an active power," he half slurred.

Leo blew out the lantern and set it and the cauldron on the counter in the kitchen before returning for Cole. "Come on. You need hydration and first aid. Luckily for you, I know a nurse."

Chapter Eighteen

WASHING the ash out of his cut hurt, though having Leo play nurse took some of the sting out. So did the ice-blue mint he took from his stash—an analgesic he usually kept on hand for the times he burned himself making candy.

"Those things aren't addictive, are they?" Leo asked, pulling on a pair of latex gloves as they sat at the kitchen table. He reached for a sterile cotton pad and the bottle of rubbing alcohol.

"Nah. Magic." Cole lifted the shoulder of his uninjured hand. "I mean, I guess long-term effects on the brain probably haven't been studied by scientists or anything. But I've never heard of anyone getting addicted. Maybe just to the candy."

"Sugar addiction is real," Leo agreed, his fingers gentle on Cole's wrist as he turned the palm up. The magic didn't numb everything, so it still hurt when Leo gently pressed on the flesh to make sure there was no ash left in the wound.

Though Leo was careful, the rubbing alcohol made Cole grimace, the harsh scent stinging his nose.

"This is pretty deep. You should probably have stitches." Leo raised his eyes to Cole's face. "And maybe ask the nurse for advice before you cut your hand for a damn blood sacrifice next time. The outside of your arm would've been better. You've seen too many dumb movies."

Cole flushed. He would have liked to say he'd picked his hand for a good reason, but in truth, he hadn't thought about it. He'd never done this sort of protection spell before—or any other kind of blood magic. "I guess I'll have to suffer." His stomach lurched a bit as Leo sterilized a needle, and he looked away out the window just as Niamh flew in.

She didn't say anything to Leo—apparently he was still on her shit list—but she cocked her head at Cole. "Really? You cut your palm?"

Leo snorted quietly but said nothing, just adjusted Cole's arm so it rested comfortably on the throw pillow he'd borrowed from the couch. "Try not to look. I'll be as gentle as I can."

Cole bit his lip and kept his eyes on Niamh, thinking about the other thing he needed to find. Something that would protect Leo when he wasn't home with Cole. Cole had never heard of an amulet so powerful that it would actively repel anyone who sought to do the wearer harm, but certain trinkets would grant some amount of luck when it came to evading such people. The problem was that most required an item of some significance—heirloom jewelry worked best, since it could usually be worn inconspicuously, but Cole didn't have any, and he wouldn't ask Gran. Items made by the spellcaster could also work, but Cole doubted any of his candies would stand up to the magic he'd need to put inside them. They'd probably melt and Leo would get a sugar burn.

"Cole?" Leo prodded.

Cole looked over without meaning to and saw that Leo had finished the stitches while he'd been thinking. Seven tiny, precise lines down the center of his palm. That gave him an idea.

"Do you have anything better than Polysporin?" Leo asked.

Actually, Cole did, somewhere in the back of his fridge, provided it hadn't spoiled.

It hadn't, and Leo applied some of the salve to Cole's cut before carefully wrapping his hand in a layer of gauze. "There," Leo said, and finished the whole thing off with a kiss to Cole's knuckles. "Finished."

Cole wanted to get started on his amulet idea, but before he could say as much, Leo yawned hugely, and Cole followed suit. Perhaps that could wait until morning. After all, they'd be safe here. "Bed?" Leo asked hopefully.

"Yes, please."

It had been a long time since Cole had shared a bed with a partner on a regular basis. He wasn't sure he'd ever done it with sex completely off the table. He thought it would be strange, brushing his teeth next to someone else, crawling into bed with them, making room in his sleep routine for another person. And it had been, a bit, the first day or two—he had double sinks in the master bath, but their elbows bumped while they brushed, and Cole liked to read the news in bed on his phone before he went to sleep, but Leo made grumbly noises at the light.

But when he closed his eyes at last, Leo's steady breathing filled his ears. Leo got him—for some strange reason Leo *loved* him. And if Cole had his way, he would never be alone again.

"I AM a genius," Cole said after breakfast, having dug a ball of yarn and a pair of needles out from where he'd stashed them in the altar room.

Leo simply raised his eyebrows before going back to the book Cole had lent him. It was old—definitely older than Cole, probably older than Gran—and discussed the theory behind simple hedge magic. Leo seemed engrossed.

"I am an idiot," Cole sighed two minutes later, setting the needles down. He couldn't do much with a slash across his palm; the bandage seriously messed with his dexterity.

This time Leo put the book down entirely. "I didn't know you knit."

Cole shrugged. "I'm not very good. Especially right now." He waved his bandaged hand. "Kate taught me years ago, said I should learn even if I'm not much of a spellcaster. And she was right, because in theory I should be able to weave a protection spell into a scarf or something—*if* I could actually use both hands."

"Hmm. Can I?" Leo asked, reaching for the yarn. Then he picked up the scissors and cut a few foot-long strands. He tied the ends together. "What if you just…?"

Cole considered. "It might work. Three-strand is probably too simple to hold it all, but let me cut a few more and see." He'd be pretty embarrassed if the protection bracelet he made his boyfriend overloaded, caught fire, and burned him.

Eventually he made it work with fourteen strands, though the ends of the bracelet weren't pretty and the whole thing looked amateur. But fourteen strands contained the spell Cole wove into it, along with a spray of lavender, without any sign of strain. He was tying it around Leo's wrist when his phone beeped.

Kate Alpin, the display informed him. Oh good. Just what Cole needed: prying questions from well-meaning family members. Probably a not-so-subtle reminder that Gran expected him at dinner today too. Well, too bad. If Gran wanted to see him, she could call him herself. Until then, Cole had better things to do.

He finished off the knot and raised his eyes to Leo's. "So," he said, "wanna play hooky?"

THE parking lot at the nature preserve had one spot remaining when they arrived, and it was a good thing they'd taken Cole's car, because Leo's SUV wouldn't have fit. Cole, though, slipped in without any trouble, feeling, ironically, a bit like a kid in the candy store.

"Why's it so busy?" Leo asked, frowning, closing the car door behind him.

Cole grabbed his hand and started tugging him toward the trail that led through the forest to the lakeshore. "You'll see."

Most of the tourists they passed coming back wore binoculars around their necks or carried expensive cameras, and they all had a certain bounce to their step. Leo cocked his head at them, but otherwise he seemed content to let Cole carry on with his surprise.

"It's nice here," Leo commented, taking in the scenery. "Nicer if it was quiet, though, maybe."

"This park is as far south as you can go in Canada. There's actually a sandbar that sticks out into the lake—well, sometimes." Cole smiled up at him. "Good place to do magic, if you have an active power." Sometimes his family rented out one of the pavilions for one of the witches' Sabbaths, especially Beltane and Lammas; the park closed too early to do the entire celebration here, but the kids loved it.

Cole didn't say that out loud, though. Thinking of his family hurt, and he didn't want to ruin their outing. So he'd turned his phone off and left it in his jacket pocket. He concentrated on Leo instead, the way their footsteps synced up, the occasional bump of their shoulders.

Today they didn't see much in the way of wildlife, aside from a handful of red-wing blackbirds and squirrels, which tended to ignore human passersby. But the dirt path squished pleasantly beneath their feet, and the crisp autumn air carried hints of lake water and rich soil, and the leaves were turning, vibrant reds and cheerful yellows mixed in with browns and greens. They had to let go of each other's hand a few times to avoid clotheslining the giggling children who scampered down the path, followed more sedately by apologetic parents, but Leo always reached for Cole again after.

Soon came the indistinct murmur of a gathered crowd, and then suddenly, as they passed out of the trees into the beachside clearing, they met a wall of backsides.

Leo stopped abruptly. "What's everybody…."

Cole smiled and followed his slack-jawed gaze up to a beech tree lit with the pulsing, vibrant orange of fall. Except it wasn't the tree's leaves that gave it the color—those were still green, little bundles almost completely obscured by fluttering black and orange.

"Are those…?" Leo asked, voice hushed.

Cole squeezed his hand. "Butterflies," he confirmed. Tens of thousands of them, so many that the tree seemed to have been set ablaze. "I told you. Monarch migration. It's a big deal."

"It's incredible," Leo murmured. "This happens every year? How do they know to come back? I didn't know butterflies lived that long."

"They don't. These ones have never been to Mexico." Cole leaned into Leo as he spoke, not wanting to disturb anyone else. For the most part, the assembled watchers kept their voices down. "But every year they gather here, and every year they find their way to the same spot in Mexico. And every spring they come back, though it takes a couple of generations. Instinctively. Wild, huh?"

"Incredible," Leo repeated, leaning his head against Cole's. "Thank you, for showing me."

Cole longed to kiss him, but maybe not here. At least not until he had a read on how Leo felt about PDA. "You're welcome."

For a few minutes they watched in silence, taking in one of nature's marvels. But for the uninitiated— which included Cole—there was only so long you could stare at a tree full of butterflies. Eventually they turned around to head back toward the hospital so Leo could pick up his car.

"Think we can stop at my apartment?" Leo asked when they were about five minutes out. "I want to get a few more things."

Cole was tempted to tell him he should get *all* of his things, but perhaps that was putting the cart before the horse. "Sure."

Leo's apartment was none the worse for wear, save the potted plant that hadn't been watered in weeks. "It's a peace lily," Cole said, filling a pitcher with water from the kitchen sink. "It'll perk up."

Leo looked dubious, but he let Cole water his plant while he went into the bedroom to pack.

Cole had just set the empty pitcher on the counter when someone knocked on the door.

"Hello?"

Apparently they hadn't closed it all the way; it swung open a few inches to reveal Nate, Leo's neighbor.

"Oh, hey, Cole." Nate's broad, open face creased in concern as he stepped into the apartment. "Is Leo here with you? I haven't seen him in a while."

"Yeah, he's just putting some things together." Cole weighed how much to say. He thought Nate was trustworthy, but then it wasn't his story to tell. "He'll be staying with me a while."

"Ooooh," Nate said, waggling his eyebrows. "Say no more. Good for you guys." Then he adopted an exaggeratedly put-upon expression, shaking his head and raising his gaze to the ceiling. "The good ones are always taken."

Cole snorted. He wasn't sure which of them Nate was referring to, but Nate was practically a puppy—far too young for Cole. "Sorry," he said, but he couldn't make it sound sincere.

Nate grinned. "It's all good, my heart will go on." Jesus, he was barely older than that song.

"Okay, I'm ready." Leo emerged from the bedroom with a small rolling suitcase and a shopping bag, and Cole went pleasantly warm all over. Apparently he meant to stay for quite some time. "Hey, Nate. You need something?"

"Nah, just checking in on you." He smiled, though this one looked a little anemic. "You kids have fun."

Nate wasn't nearly far enough away when Leo shook his head. "He's a weird one."

"That's one way of putting it," Cole agreed mildly. Nate would probably find it funny. "Come on. You can make me dinner, and then I'll let you take advantage of me."

"Now who could resist an offer like that?"

Chapter Nineteen

LEO knew Cole was keeping something from him. The number of times he'd received a notification on his phone only to shove it away or turn it off entirely.... Well, Leo might have let it slide once or twice, but he'd been doing it constantly for a week. Then, on Sunday evening, for the second week in a row, he skipped dinner at his grandmother's.

Leo got the impression that whatever had happened between Cole and his grandmother—and it must have been something, to send Cole home early Friday night—had led to some hard feelings. Leo didn't want to pry and risk bursting the warm, happy bubble of their first few days together.

Monday morning, though, Leo had to go back to work—he was on days until Friday, meaning he was up and out of the house before the sun. He was used to that—to leaving a lover sleeping soundly when he got up for work—but the empty space on the bed next to Cole tempted him sorely.

Work, though. And he wanted to catch up with Jimmy. He packed Niamh into the car and set off.

For the first three hours of his shift, Leo kept his head down and steered clear of the many attempts to engage him in gossip about what had happened last Saturday. He hoped their coworkers weren't pestering Jimmy.

Finally he got a break and snuck down to say hello.

Outside room 2117 sat a chair, empty except for a newspaper. Leo supposed the police had decided whoever had hurt Jimmy wasn't going to come back, and they were at least half-right—as long as the sun was up, Jimmy should be safe.

The door was open. Leo knocked on the frame and stuck his head inside.

Someone had drawn the curtains around the bed closest to the window, but Jimmy was sitting up in the bed closest to Leo. He looked healthy—good color, unlabored breathing, and no IV or catheter. He'd be getting discharged any minute now. But when Leo knocked, he raised his head sharply before groaning. "I just had my vitals taken five minutes ago."

Yeah, seemed like he was going to be fine. Physically, at least. "Relax. I'm on my break. See?" He held out his arms. He'd thrown a hoodie on over his scrubs in hopes of warding off requests from any patients or their visitors.

Unfortunately this didn't placate Jimmy. "Are you here to grill me about last Saturday, then?" He softened slightly. "Dr. Stivali said you were the one who got to me first, so. Thanks for that." He turned his head just slightly. "But I don't really remember much."

A lie, Leo thought, reaching for the curtain around the bed. He didn't want to be interrupted. "Actually, I am here to talk about that," he said. "But instead of asking all the questions, maybe I can fill you in on a few things."

Jimmy watched him close the curtains. "Really," he said, so guardedly it came out as a statement rather than a question. "Like what?"

Now they had the illusion of privacy, Leo took the chair next to Jimmy's bed. "Well, for starters, I know the guy who left you at the ER. Guy by the name of Roman Dvorak. Ring a bell?"

From the way Jimmy avoided his gaze, Leo thought maybe it did. Perhaps Jimmy knew more than Leo had anticipated.

But how much more?

"I don't know how well you know him," Leo continued as tactfully as he could, cataloging Jimmy's every twitch, "how much you know about him and the kind of guy he is…."

Now Jimmy speared him with an intense look. "Roman didn't do this to me."

So they did know each other! "And I'm sure he didn't leave you shivering in the shower the other night either," Leo said acidly.

Jimmy huffed. "Yeah, he left me in the shower to get warm. This is a hospital! He knew someone would find me and help me. But he's not the one who b—"

Jackpot. "Not the one who what?" Leo prompted softly.

Jimmy gritted his teeth and looked away.

Looked like Leo would have to be the one to come clean. "Not the one who bit you," he said, and Jimmy's mouth dropped open.

"How did you… you *know*?"

"About…." Leo paused, listening for any activity from the bed by the window. Nothing. "About vampires?" *And witches and curses and God knows what else?* "Yeah, Jimmy, I know. You're not the only one in this room who's been an appetizer."

"Think I was the main course," Jimmy said ruefully—a fair point. "Anyway, what have you got against Roman? He's the only reason I'm still breathing and not, you know, decomposing in a soybean field somewhere."

Now Leo stared, agape. "What?"

"He saved my life," Jimmy said firmly. "Man, how many vampires do you know? Because this other guy—I've learned my lesson, okay? No Tinder dates who refuse to meet me during daylight hours."

Finally things started to make sense. "Other guy?" Leo repeated.

"Yeah. Kyle."

"Kyle?" Fine, Leo was starting to sound like a broken record, but who ever heard of a vampire named *Kyle*?

Apparently Jimmy agreed with him. "I know, right? I guess he's kind of new at the whole, uh, you know." He lowered his voice. "Bloodsucking thing. No self-control. Roman's been trying to"—his face twisted as though he were working not to laugh—"take him under his wing? But, you know. I guess it's like going through vampire puberty or something."

Leo had come into this meeting expecting to provide some answers, but instead he kept finding more questions. "So… who left you the money, then? After Kyle bit you in the hospital."

"Roman. Must've been. I guess he was trying to throw you off? Since it seems like you know him." Jimmy narrowed his eyes, looking Leo up and down in an obvious effort to determine exactly how *well* Leo knew him.

In for a penny. "Ex-boyfriend. I guess he could've been. Or maybe it was hush money."

Jimmy smoothed a hand over his neck. "He should know I don't need that. He probably overheard me talking about getting those winter tires."

Oh boy. Leo wasn't sure what to say to that, so he decided to leave it alone. "Well, if you… you know. If things don't go well and you need help, just… you can ask me."

"Yeah?" That assessing look returned with a renewed focus. "What makes you such an expert, huh?"

My boyfriend is a witch. But Leo couldn't say that; he'd taken Cole's example about not outing other obscures to heart, and he especially wouldn't do it when he was talking to another human. "I know some people," he said instead. "They know all kinds of stuff I don't. But I guess they're invested in people not getting hurt."

Jimmy raised skeptical eyebrows.

"Okay, that sounded hokey," Leo admitted. "But look, I went through something sort of similar to what you are, okay? And I lucked into getting someone who actually wanted to help me. And he'll help you too, if you need it. We don't want to see you get hurt. You know, worse than the two attempted exsanguinations."

That, at least, got a small laugh. "God. Vampires, right?"

"Man, you have no idea."

Leo had to go back on duty shortly after, but he did so feeling lighter, even if he had more questions than ever. Were Jimmy and Roman involved? Had he really misunderstood Roman's involvement in the whole thing? Was Roman not responsible for cursing Leo after all?

But it was hard to care too much about any of it. The curse was broken, Jimmy had recovered enough to be released and even go back to work, and Leo had Cole waiting for him at home, at least metaphorically. Work passed quickly, even when the rest of the gossip dried up and Leo had to field questions about the guy who'd picked him up last week.

"I started staying with him when my apartment had to be fumigated," Leo said, reciting the lie he'd been feeding everyone from the beginning.

"And you just decided to stay forever?" Deborah teased.

Leo's cheeks heated at *forever*, but he stood his ground. "I was invited," he said loftily, and everyone laughed.

He stopped for groceries on the way home; Cole would still be at work for another hour or two, so Leo might as well get started making dinner. They were out of coffee as well, so he stopped at Caffeine for some of Cole's favorite roast. Across the street, next to the flower shop, the For Lease sign had come down and someone was unloading some kind of industrial-looking equipment.

"You know what's going in across the street?" Leo asked as he handed Andre his debit card.

Andre shook his head, running the card through the reader before passing the terminal over. "No idea. Sign came down this morning. Someone must be in a hurry, I guess."

Leo keyed in his PIN. "Seems like."

Andre hummed. "Hey, I thought you liked the french roast. Was the last batch no good or something?"

"Oh. Um, no." Leo's ears heated. "Cole likes this one, though, so. I guess it's growing on me?"

"Really?" Andre said. Then he shook his head cheerfully. "Well, good for both of you. Here, take a couple cookies to celebrate. Certified no hazelnuts."

Leo put away the groceries still thinking about what was eating Cole and was about to ask Niamh when he actually looked at the calendar stuck to the front of the fridge and answered his own question. October 31 was outlined in orange, with *Gran's* written diagonally across the square, a little party hat sitting jauntily over the *a*.

What was it Cole had said once about Samhain? Something about wild family parties. But Cole hadn't mentioned anything about going to Gran's next week.

Whatever was going on, Leo had the crawling suspicion Gran was right at the center of it.

BY the twenty-fifth, Cole hadn't decided what to do about Samhain. He could observe it by himself, but it wouldn't feel right. Or he could contact another coven and take part in their festivities. But then he wouldn't be able to bring Leo—witches understandably felt strongly about being outed to mundanes who had no particular attachment to them—and he didn't know that that would be any better. He'd probably spend the whole evening moping.

At least he had work to distract him. Samhain was a celebration for more than just witches, and Danielle kept just as busy in the front of the shop as Cole did in the back, creating the usual Halloween favorites, caramels and vampire lips, gumballs shaped like eyes, and candy corn—*good* candy corn, fresh and soft and fragrant. Leo kept commenting that Cole smelled like candy floss, which so far had only led to good things for Cole.

Until now. Waiting for the sugar to boil, he got lost in a reverie thinking about last night, when Leo set about testing whether Cole tasted as good as he smelled (Leo said yes; Cole suspected he was embellishing but appreciated the sentiment). The next thing he knew, the sugar was way too hot for what he wanted. He guessed he was making another batch of caramels. He adjusted the temperature to make sure the sugar didn't burn and went to grab the cream and butter.

He was watching the caramel set in the pan—a bit like watching paint dry, except a better experience for the nose—when the bell above the door in the front of the shop jingled. A moment later Danielle popped her head back. "Amy stopped in for a chat. You busy?"

Cole was not, and was in fact becoming a danger to himself in the kitchen, so he hung his apron on the peg behind the door and decamped to the shopfront. "Candy emergency?" he asked.

"Ugh." Amy threw herself onto one of the stools at the counter and looked over at him. "Just finished organizing a last-minute Halloween party for this weekend. Do you have anything with caffeine in it?"

Cole snorted but grabbed a jar of coffee candies from the shelf behind the register and used the tongs to pick out a few. "Why didn't you just go to Andre's?"

Amy slid him a toonie. "I would have had to cross the street again. I wandered over to peek in the window at the new place on the corner. The things that man is doing to cocoa powder…." She shot him a guilty look as she paused with a coffee candy halfway to her mouth. "No offense."

Cole waved it off and put the toonie in the till. "None taken. I don't do chocolate."

"Yes, as I've previously lamented." She popped the candy in her mouth and made a pleased noise. "Now I can have the best of both worlds."

What a choice of words. "Wish I could do the same," Cole said before he could stop himself.

Amy straightened up and tilted her head. "What's that mean?" Then her eyes widened. "You're not having second thoughts about—"

So Leo had updated her on his relationship status. Cole shook his head. "No, no, I'm…. That's not it at all. I—" *love Leo.* Nope, too soon to be telling Amy if he hadn't said it to Leo, and she'd probably think he was nuts anyway. They'd only known each other a few weeks.

Amy raised an eyebrow.

"My grandmother's being kind of difficult," he finally said. Even with the protections on the shop—he'd warded against scrying, partly out of habit and partly because Gran was a notorious busybody and Cole enjoyed the illusion of privacy—he avoided saying anything too negative out loud, lest she somehow overhear.

"Difficult how?"

Cole let out a long breath. Danielle had gone on break, presumably to give him some privacy, so he might as well tell the truth and get it off his chest. "I don't, uh. I don't know if she's going to approve of me and Leo, and I don't know what I'll do if she doesn't."

Amy's face crumpled in sympathy. "Oh, Cole."

"It's fine!" he told her quickly. "I'm almost thirty years old. I shouldn't need my family's approval to do something that makes me happy."

"No, but that doesn't mean not having it doesn't hurt." They stared at each other for a moment, untangling the sentence. "Did I say that right? You know what I mean. Families are complicated."

"You have no idea."

"Have you talked to her about it?"

Guilt squirmed in Cole's gut. "Well… sort of." When she looked skeptical, but apparently was too polite to call his bullshit to his face, he went on, "I tried last Friday, only everything went sort of pear-shaped."

"I can imagine," she said. "What happened?"

He tried to laugh, but it hurt coming out. "Oh, you know how these things go. You start being real for two seconds and suddenly you can't stop and the next thing you know you're running away to your car, holding back tears like any mature adult."

"I'm so sorry. That sounds awful."

"I mean, it directly led to me making up my mind to finally kiss Leo, so it wasn't all bad." Cole didn't regret standing up for himself, but maybe he could have found a way that didn't involve storming out on his grandmother and potentially damaging their relationship.

"Still. You've always been close with your grandmother."

And he would be again, maybe. If one of them ever apologized.

"Cole?" Amy prompted.

He shook his head. "Sorry. I guess I'm not very good company today."

"Meh. Everyone has off days." She smiled sympathetically, then glanced at the clock and heaved a sigh. "I'd better get home or my cat will give me the cold shoulder."

"Can't have that." Cole followed her gaze, realizing that his own house wouldn't be empty except for Niamh. Leo would be home by now, expecting him, maybe even with dinner on. Amazing how quickly Cole had gotten used to that, and to throwing Leo's clothes in with his when he did laundry.

Amazing how thinking about it immediately made him feel better. "I think I'll follow you out."

"That's the spirit," Amy said, with the sort of cleverly camouflaged smirk that said she guessed at the reason for his sudden lighter mood. "I'll see you later, then. Have a good night!"

Cheeky, Cole thought. But he let it pass with a wave. "I will." And he was pretty sure he would.

LEO got home half an hour later than he'd expected due to an accident on the main highway that he didn't yet know how to navigate around. One of these days he'd get Cole to teach him how to get around on the back roads, or break down and buy an aftermarket navigation system. But he'd done too many ER rotations to dare trying to program his cell phone GPS while he was behind the wheel.

When he pulled into the driveway, he noticed a pristine Cadillac he'd never seen before parked at the curb in front of the neighbor's house—a late-fifties or early-sixties model, in that distinctive midcentury aqua. He was so busy checking it out on the way up to the house that he didn't notice the woman standing on the doorstep until he nearly ran into her.

She stood about five and a half feet, though her slight hunch told Leo she'd once been taller. She was built as sturdily as the car, and though wrinkles lined her face and age spots dotted her skin, Leo could tell she'd been beautiful in her youth—was beautiful still. She had her grandson's eyes, and when she smiled at him, he could see that she still had all of her teeth, and he kind of wanted to make the sign of the cross.

But he didn't even know if that worked on vampires, never mind witches, and maybe it was culturally insensitive. Instead he just said, "Uh, hi."

What was she doing here? Was this some kind of weird Alpin family thing Leo was just going to have to get used to?

"You must be Leon," she said in an even, sure tone. Her piercing gaze seemed to go right *through* him, as though she were trying to judge the quality of his internal organs. For a second he tried to remember if he'd had anything more nutritious than coffee and a granola bar, in case she decided to pick on his stomach contents.

"That's me." Automatically, he held out his hand. "But everyone calls me Leo."

"Hmm," said Gran, extending her own. "You can call me Irene, for now."

They shook. Irene's hand was warm, a little leathery but strong. "Nice to meet you, Irene."

She held on for slightly too long and maintained eye contact until Leo felt uncomfortable. But he didn't dare look away first.

"I'm afraid Cole's not here, though, if you're looking for him," he went on. His voice held a definite note of *so you can grovel an apology and beg him for mercy for whatever you did to him*, even though she scared the bejeezus out of him. Something about her felt familiar, like they'd met before, but no. He'd definitely remember.

"Actually, I came to speak with you." She withdrew her hand and broke eye contact, though Leo somehow didn't feel as if he'd won that contest. "May I come in?"

Ever since the whole vampire ex-boyfriend thing, Leo was wary of inviting people into homes, but he didn't see a way to refuse politely, and from what Cole had said, Irene could turn him into a frog on a whim. "Of course." He unlocked the door and allowed her to step past him into the house. "Would you like something to drink? Tea?"

It was strange, navigating the waters between *you hurt Cole and I'm not going to let you do it again* and *please like me, it's important to him*. He didn't like it.

"That herbal one Cole keeps in the old Twinings tin." She didn't take off her shoes, but if ninetysomethings didn't get a pass from unnecessary bending, Leo didn't know who did.

"Sure." He busied himself with the tea routine. Was this a witch thing, he wondered, or a Cole's family thing? Maybe in a few weeks he'd be a convert himself. Certainly it had helped the night Jimmy was attacked. Perhaps the British were on to something. "What did you want to talk about?"

"I'd like you to come to Friday dinner tomorrow."

Leo almost dropped the tea tin. Cole had made it pretty clear that Friday dinner was a sacred ritual as far as his grandmother was concerned. "Oh?" he said, hoping to buy time to come up with a response that wasn't an endless string of question marks.

Irene made a noise then, a long, deep, pitchless exhale through the nose. Leo poured the hot water and set the teapot on its trivet on the table to steep, then sat across from her and waited.

Finally she raised her eyes from the teapot. "When Cole was a boy," she began, but then she faltered and started again. "Cole was never like my other grandchildren."

Yeah, Leo knew all about that. "So I've been told."

Irene shook her head. "He was always more sensitive. More inquisitive. More in tune with his cousins than the rest."

Leo blinked off his surprise—not at what she'd said, but that she was the one who said it. "That sounds about right." He hoped she wasn't going to ruin the goodwill she'd earned by implying any of that was due to Cole being gay.

"That's still true of him today. Even now, of all my grandchildren, Cole is the most centered, the least capricious. He grew from a good boy—don't get me wrong, he got into plenty of trouble, but never because he was cruel—into a good man." She pulled the mug Leo had placed on the table toward her and peered into it as though inspecting for dust, but she didn't reach for the teapot yet. Instead she met Leo's eyes and said, "And I've been afraid of losing him."

"Losing him?"

"I thought, when he was a boy, that he would be the perfect heir if only he could practice magic. I'd half made up my mind to name him anyway. And then when he was a teenager…." She shook her head. "Of course his power is cursebreaking. I don't know why I ever thought it would be any different."

Something didn't add up, though. If Irene was afraid of losing Cole, what had happened two weeks ago to make him leave her place early? "Is this about why Cole has been avoiding you?"

"In a way." Irene put the mug down and rubbed her hands together, massaging the palm of one hand down to the fingers and repeating with the other. "Has he told you much about us? Witches, magic, our beliefs?"

"Some." Leo had read the book on hedge magic, and he'd taken in as much as he could about magic, energy, water, life. He knew he'd only scratched the surface. "I know about the Sabbaths and about the lakes. His candies."

She nodded. "Has he explained the balance of the universe?"

Sometimes the universe likes things a certain way. "A little bit," Leo hedged. "I didn't really understand."

"For witches, it's very important to keep the universe in balance. The smallest action can have unforeseen consequences. And the universe has been clear with

Cole that as much as he might love any of his previous boyfriends—or the idea of them—they weren't for him."

Leo would have gone batshit in half a second. He stared. "Seriously?" Hadn't Cole said he once got strep throat when he was supposed to break up with someone? "'The universe,' though? You guys have kind of high opinions of yourselves. No offense, but that sounds like some New Age bullshit."

To his surprise, Irene laughed, a short, sharp bark of sound. "We're witches, dear. 'Some New Age bullshit' covers a lot of sins. Eventually we all learn how to want something badly enough to tell the universe to shove it. It's a rite of passage. Until then, it's a good exercise in mindfulness."

She sobered again. "I have the Sight, as I'm sure Cole has told you. He's always craved reassurance that he wouldn't be alone forever, and I haven't been able to give it to him. We clairvoyants, we're not supposed to interfere directly." Her lips thinned and she looked down at her mug. "But that's not easy to stick to, or to accept."

Leo watched her for a second more. He didn't know her, but she seemed genuinely upset, distraught at the idea that she'd hurt her relationship with her only grandson. Gently, he retrieved the mug and filled it with tea before setting it back down. "And now you want to make it right."

"Well, as I said, sometimes we have to tell the universe to shove it. My reticence on the subject was… shortsighted," she admitted with a wry twist of her mouth.

Leo found himself laughing helplessly, knowing her gifts as he did. "Oh God. Cole gets his sense of humor from you."

Irene laughed too, easier this time, putting one hand over her mouth. "He does. I'm sorry. Those T-shirts—they are wonderful. Every time I see a good one, I have to buy it for him."

"Don't apologize!" Leo said, scandalized. "I love them!"

Oh. Oh, his ears were turning red. His whole *body* was turning red, because it wasn't just the puns he'd admitted to loving.

He was trying to think of something else to say when Irene reached across the table and patted his hand. "I can see that, dear. I wouldn't have invited you for dinner otherwise."

Leo gave up trying to decide whether he ought to be embarrassed. If Irene thought he should be, she would let him know. That much he felt sure of. "Well," he said, still a little awkward. "Just as long as I know where I stand."

"As long as you're standing with my grandson, I think we'll get along fine."

Leo couldn't help the blush this time either.

Irene didn't stick around long after that. She didn't even finish her tea, just thanked Leo for the hospitality and kissed his cheek as she left. Part of Leo wondered if that was some kind of spell, and he guessed he wouldn't know until Cole came home. Irene gave a jaunty wave from her aquamarine Cadillac and drove off with a dainty toot of her horn.

Leo waved too, frankly mystified, and then went back inside. There was still enough tea in the teapot for another mug, so he poured one for himself and sat inhaling the steam, relaxing as the warmth seeped through him.

Damn. That was some good shit. Leo needed more tea in his life. Maybe it would even taste good? He raised it to his lips and tested it.

Hmm. Not bad. Not too sweet, a little fruity, a little…
leafy. It was still tea. But just like the tea the night after
Jimmy had been attacked, this soothed him. And he needed
soothing. Meeting Cole's nutty, overbearing witch of a
grandmother on the fly, on his own, had him pretty tense.

The tea, though. The tea loosened his shoulders
and made his legs sprawl. It made his head lean to the
side. This shit was magic.

Oh shit, it was magic. Leo drank magic tea.

His lips twitched involuntarily, and then a little sound
escaped them. Then another one, louder. He giggled for a
handful of seconds, then tried to take another sip of tea but
only managed to sputter because he was still laughing.

After a minute or so the giggles passed. He should
get up and clean the pot, put the dishes in the dishwasher,
start dinner. But what if he just sat at the kitchen table and
stared at the ceiling?

Huh. Now that he was looking, it could use a coat
of paint.

He didn't know how long he'd been sitting there, but
the tea was gone when the front door opened. "Leo?"

"In the kitchen." Oops. Hopefully Leo wasn't in
trouble for drinking the special tea.

Cole walked in a second later, wearing the Fruitier
Than a Nutcake shirt and smelling like fresh caramel.
Yum. "Hey, have you—youuuuu have had visitors."

Maybe he was in trouble for letting Irene in the
house instead. "Your grandmother is either not as scary
as you think she is," Leo said, then paused for several
seconds while he considered. "Or else she's way scarier
than you think she is."

"The latter," Cole said, sliding into the seat Irene had
vacated a few moments before. "What did she want? Other
than to get you stoned on my special blend?"

"She invited me to dinner tomorrow." Leo heard his voice as though someone else were speaking. He sounded dreamy. But—wait. He looked up sharply. "I didn't start drinking it until she left! How was I supposed to know your gran partakes in… *special blend*!"

"It's good for her hypertension," Cole said, defensive. Then: "She really invited you for dinner?"

Leo nodded, then realized when the room spun that he needed to stop nodding. "She misses you, she was wrong to be a dickweed, she is sorry not sorry for buying you all those punny T-shirts, and she hopes we'll give her a lot of fat great-grandbabies." He lolled his head to the side and then raised it to look at Cole. "I'm paraphrasing."

"I hope so. These are not childbearing hips."

There was nothing wrong with Cole's hips, and Leo said as much.

Cole laughed. "How long did you let that stuff steep, anyway?"

"Steep time is a factor?" That could explain why Irene had kept it together while Leo was orbiting Saturn.

"I'll make you some coffee," Cole offered, standing. He pressed a kiss to Leo's crown as he walked by.

"Do you have to?" Leo leaned back and watched Cole's butt as he went by. It was a good butt. Round. Squeezable. "I mean, am I gonna get a magic hangover, ooooor?"

Cole turned around before he could reach for the kettle. "No, it'll let you down gently in a half an hour or so."

Nodding, Leo stood, forcibly reminded himself to stop nodding, and held out his arms. "Then come cuddle me for half an hour, and after that you can explain why you have mind-altering tea unlabeled in your cupboard."

They snuggled on the couch for a few minutes, but enough time must have passed that Leo was already coming out of it, because the fuzzy pleasantness soon became more focused. "So we're gonna go to dinner, right?" he said, tilting his head back in Cole's lap.

Cole carded his fingers through Leo's hair, raising goose bumps on his neck. "You want to?"

"I mean, if your grandmother isn't gonna eat me alive while we're alone together, she probably isn't going to try anything while you're actually present." Leo stretched his neck a little, hoping to entice Cole's fingers lower, to his nape. It worked; he sighed blissfully. "Besides, I think she likes me."

The fingers paused. "I can't decide if that's comforting."

Good point. Still. "Are you happy?"

Cole found a place on Leo's neck that made his spine liquefy and his toes tingle. "More than I ever thought I would be."

That took care of the last of the fuzziness. Leo felt everything in sharp relief now, and the warmth had migrated firmly south. Sitting up, he caught Cole's hand and pulled him to his feet. "More than you ever thought you would be. Let's see if we can do better."

Chapter Twenty

"YOU'RE sure it's okay I invited Amy?"

Cole rolled his eyes, shoving another Tupperware of candy into a reusable shopping bag. "Yes, I'm sure. Gran's Samhain celebration is a neighborhood thing, not just a family thing. Plenty of mundanes not in the know. Besides, what were you going to do, uninvite her?"

Leo rubbed his palms on his jeans. "Sorry. I just…. It's possible I'm nervous about meeting your entire family. At one time. Knowing they're all witches."

"Gran is the scariest, and you already met her. Everyone else is a cinch." He paused. "Well, no. Aunt June's husband is a piece of work. His name is Todd. Stay out of his way."

"Is he a witch?"

"No, he's just insufferable." And sometimes a little too persuasive when it came to getting Aunt June to use her magic to his advantage. Cole hefted the bag and took one last look around the kitchen to make sure they had everything. "Self-righteous, entitled, blah blah blah."

Leo made a face. "Thanks for the warning." He picked up his own bag—he'd made a pumpkin stew, very in keeping with the theme—and followed Cole to the front door. "Other than Uncle Todd, anything I need to watch out for?"

"Try not to combine too much candy with alcohol. Oh, and after the muggles go home, we all dance naked around the fire."

Cole was opening the door when he said it, so he didn't see Leo's face, but he *did* hear him trip. He turned around; there was nothing on the floor. Leo's eyes were doing a fair impression of the eyeball jawbreakers Cole had made for a Halloween special.

Cole laughed. "Come on. We don't want to be late."

Today street parking in front of Gran's offered limited options. Cole slid into a spot half a block down and put the car in Park. He'd done the same countless other times, Fridays and Sundays and witches' Sabbaths. But today didn't feel like those other days.

Today he felt....

"Oh, hey, there's Amy," Leo said, pointing.

Cole's heart sped—not quite a gallop, but maybe a canter. "Why don't you go say hello?" That would give Cole a minute to center himself without Leo seeing how bad this freaked him out. He didn't want Leo to think he had second thoughts. He didn't. But he'd never introduced anyone to his family either, and Gran's overture notwithstanding, he didn't know how it was going to go.

Perhaps Leo understood, because he leaned over and pecked Cole's cheek. "I'll go meet up with her and we'll be along. Take your time."

Cole's family, however, wasn't going to allow him the luxury. "Uncle Cole!" As soon as he closed the car door, Ella hit his knees doing forty kilometers an hour and knocked the apprehension right out of him. "You're pink today!"

And now a six-year-old was making him blush with comments on his emotional state. Talk about whiplash. "Princess!" he crowed, scooping her up and tossing her in the air. "Pink? Really?"

"Uh-huh." Ella planted a wet kiss on his cheek. "But I'm not a princess, Uncle Cole."

"Oh no?" He set her down again, grabbed the bags from the back of the car, and took her hand as they walked toward Gran's.

"I'm an astronaut!" Sure enough, she wore a bright orange jumpsuit with NASA stitched on the pocket. He imagined that somewhere in Gran's yard was an abandoned fishbowl helmet with several large breathing holes drilled into it. "I am a strong, innapennet girl. And strong, innapennet girls are astronauts."

Oh boy. That was her mother talking, all right. Not that she didn't have a point. But: "You don't think princesses have to be strong and independent?"

Ella chewed on that as they walked up the porch steps. "Can I be a princess *and* an astronaut?"

"Kid, if anyone can, it's you." She'd probably have someone making her a crown in the next twenty minutes.

They reached the knee-high picket fence around Gran's yard, and Ella abandoned him for the other kids. Half the neighborhood and then some appeared to be here already—Cole saw Nate and Andre, and Mrs. Hudson from three doors down, and someone dressed as a unicorn who might be his third-grade teacher.

"No costume?"

Cole whirled to his left; Kate wore, as she did every year, a maxi dress with a jagged hem, numerous pentacle necklaces, and a shoulder bag full of yarn and needles—a "stitchin' witch," she called it.

Their whole family was doomed to enjoy terrible wordplay.

"I came as an emotionally mature adult," he said. He'd even texted her yesterday to apologize for avoiding her. Then he handed over his bounty. "Here, I brought ten pounds of candy."

Kate took the bag and was in the middle of rolling her eyes when something over Cole's shoulder caught her eye. Uncle Todd passed them by just then, and she caught his arm and gave him the task of bringing the candy to the porch for setup. For once Uncle Todd didn't argue; Cole thought he might be a little afraid of Kate the way more sensible people feared Gran.

When he'd gone, Kate jerked her head toward the sidewalk. "Is that who I think it is?"

Cole turned.

Leo and Amy were walking up the sidewalk together. Amy had dressed up too: a black dress with a purple sash, purple striped socks, buckle shoes with curled-up toes. She'd drawn her eyebrows pointy and chosen a dramatic maroon lipstick, but the effect came across as cheerful and fun.

Leo was wearing a T-shirt he'd bought just for the occasion. He had the pot of pumpkin stew tucked under one muscular arm, and the shirt was in danger of rucking up, making it difficult to read the slogan: Witch Better Have My Candy. His blond hair practically sparkled in the sun, and his skin glowed, and if someone had told Cole right then that Leo had elf blood somewhere in his family tree, he'd have believed them.

"That's my boyfriend," he said, grinning stupidly.

In the yard and on the porch, adult activity seemed to stop, though the children continued their game, laughing and shouting, oblivious.

"Everyone's staring at us," Amy observed as they came within easy conversing distance.

"Everyone's staring at *him*," Kate corrected, nodding at Leo. "Cole's never brought a boy home before. Love your shoes, by the way. I'm Kate."

If possible, Amy brightened further. "Thanks! I'm Amy." She held out her package. "I figured Cole had candy covered, so I stopped by the new place in town and convinced the proprietor to give me some chocolate samples."

They led the way to the porch, already fast friends.

"Amy fits in better than I do," Leo joked.

Cole laced their fingers together. "Don't be silly. Kate will initiate you properly later. She's just giving us time to acclimate."

"By 'initiate'…?"

Cole shrugged. "Don't ask me. Like she said, I've never brought a boy home before." They reached the porch, and Cole ducked under one of the folding tables so he could plug in the slow cooker to keep the stew warm. "So. Who do you want to meet first?"

"Not Todd," Leo said immediately, and Cole would've laughed, but he was too busy making shushing noises because Todd was only a few feet away. He pointed. "Oh shit," Leo said, much quieter. Fortunately Todd was busy regaling anyone who would listen (and several who looked desperate to get away) with tales of his exploits as an insurance salesman, and didn't seem to have noticed.

Cousin Julie and Aunt June greeted Leo warmly. Ella exclaimed, "He's pink too! I like him," but couldn't be convinced to stick around longer than that, too busy being a space princess. Eventually they made their way back to Kate and Amy, now deep in discussion about the merits of chili chocolate.

"Is now a better time?" Cole teased, tugging Leo along with him.

"Now is the *best* time," Kate said. She had a smudge of chocolate at the corner of her mouth. "I'm cheating on your candy."

Amy looked up at him with a flash of guilt as she licked chocolate from her thumb. "This is so good."

Cole made formal introductions, and Kate and Leo shook hands. The world didn't end. It was all very... *normal*—the kind of normal Cole had longed for most of his life. So when Leo made hopeful eyes at the chocolate box, he just laughed and shook his head. "Come on, I promise not to be offended if you eat the chocolate."

Leo took his time choosing—each chocolate had its own shape, from tiny birds to cats to a miniscule broomstick. Leo picked a pumpkin.

"Oh my God," Leo moaned, and Cole went hot all over. "This is delicious."

Cole vowed not to be jealous and asked Amy to pass him the bowl of candy corn instead. It was still nearly as fresh as the day he'd made it, and it melted in his mouth, even if it wasn't as good as the chocolate smelled. But after a few seconds, he started feeling... strange.

"Cole?"

Cole licked his lips. They tingled. His tongue grew thick as his vision darkened. His fingers throbbed.

"Oh shit," Kate said as though from far away, and the bowl of candy corn spilled as it dropped from Cole's nerveless fingers. "Are they—I can't see any curses—"

Had she just casually outed magic in front of Amy as though it didn't matter? Cole wanted to rebuke her, but he couldn't seem to take in air. His lungs itched, but his throat had swollen. He managed only a thin, pathetic breath.

"No, it's—hazelnuts, he's allergic to hazelnuts—there must've been some in the chocolate. It was on Amy's fingers—"

Cole swayed, sure he was about to fall, but strong arms caught him before he could topple.

"Amy, call 911."

He knew those chocolates were up to no good. Cole closed his eyes. They were heavy, and not being able to see with his eyes open freaked him out. His heart pounded.

Someone squeezed his hand. "Stay with me, okay? I'll be right back."

Cole didn't have the strength to squeeze back. As soon as the hand was gone, he passed out.

Chapter Twenty-One

LEO couldn't afford to hate hospitals. Fortunately, as of yet, he didn't have a reason to. But he was getting pretty tired of the visitor's chair.

It had taken him a few seconds to recognize the signs of anaphylaxis, and another few to remember Cole kept an EpiPen in the car. He'd never run so fast in his life, swearing to himself with every step that he'd learn to sew and put a damn EpiPen pocket in every piece of clothing Cole owned.

Cole was stable now, though. Expected to make a full recovery so that Leo could yell at him. But he hadn't woken yet in sixteen hours, and even though he hadn't had a secondary reaction, Leo's butt was glued to this uncomfortable blue vinyl chair while he watched the cardiac monitor.

Knock knock knock.

"Hey," Nate said from the doorway. He was holding a bouquet of daisies in pink and orange. "How is he? Any change?"

Leo shook his head. "Doctors think he should wake up soon, though." Being in the blue vinyl chair gave him a new appreciation for his patients' loved ones. Leo had medical training and all the experience in the world telling him Cole would likely be fine, but he hadn't eaten or slept or left Cole's side since their arrival. He couldn't.

Nate set the bouquet on the windowsill, which was already overflowing with gifts from other well-wishers. Leo had thrown the one with assorted chocolates in the garbage, even though it didn't contain hazelnuts. Uncle Todd had a warped sense of humor. "Well, when he wakes up, will you thank him for me? I didn't get to him in person yesterday."

Leo frowned. "Thank him?"

Nate nodded sheepishly. "Yeah. I have kind of a, um. A medical condition?"

Then Nate should be seeing a doctor, not a witch. Unless this was like the candies that helped with nausea? Or maybe he had anxiety and Cole prepared him some of that special blend. "Oh," Leo said carefully, not wanting to assume anything aloud lest he spill Cole's secret.

Nate nodded. "Yeah. And like, it's fine, most of the time I don't snore! But I guess wolf-me didn't get that memo, because Cole gave me a recording of what I sound like when the moon is full, and man, I am *loud*. So. Sorry if I woke you, by the way, back before you moved in with him."

Leo's lips moved soundlessly as he parsed that. *Wolf-me. Full moon. Snoring.* "That was *you*?" he finally said, reeling. That trilling, eerie, rumbly noise that had rattled things in his apartment had been his *werewolf neighbor snoring*. And Cole had known about it! "You uh—you just sleep through the full moon?"

"I walk dogs starting at six." Nate shrugged. "Wolves are good at sleeping."

Wolves are good at sleeping. Leo was going to start keeping a diary of all the insane things he had learned. "Right. That makes sense." He shook it off. "I'll tell him you stopped by."

"Thanks." Nate glanced at his watch. "Well, since he's not awake, I might as well see if they need me at the shelter. See you later, Leo."

Leo waved him off, shaking his head internally. He wondered how long it would be before revelations like this became commonplace. Maybe one day he'd even start anticipating them.

He must have spaced out, hypnotized by the beep and whir of the monitors, because he about hit the ceiling when Cole wheezed, "Wow, you look terrible."

"Cole!" Leo turned to look at him, taking in the dark circles on his face and the glassy sheen to his eyes. The steady, perfect rise and fall of his chest as he breathed, unassisted. "You look beautiful."

Cole laughed weakly as Leo took his hand. "Liar."

Leo had never meant anything so much in his life. He kissed the back of Cole's hand. "Amy sends her profuse apologies. I guess the chocolate guy had hired someone to help him set up, and they mixed up the chocolates. They're fired now, which doesn't help you, but still."

Cole groaned. "It's my own fault. I should know to be more careful around strange chocolates." He took a couple of deep breaths; apparently talking was still a lot of work for his overtaxed lungs. "That'll teach me not to carry my EpiPen."

"I ordered five," Leo admitted.

"Course you did." Cole smiled weakly, closing his eyes. "For the record, anaphylaxis sucks. Do not recommend."

"Noted." Leo squeezed his hand. "Get some rest, okay? I love you." The words came easily now, after everything that had happened. Leo wouldn't risk leaving them unsaid.

Cole didn't open his eyes again, but his smile was stronger this time, and he squeezed back. "Love you too."

IT was a strange thing, having your ninety-two-year-old grandmother visit you in the hospital. Despite their recent reconciliation, Cole didn't think he was going to like it.

Still, years of self-preservation instinct kept him polite. "Hi, Gran." He could sit up under his own power now, more than twenty-four hours after his attack. He itched to go home, take a shower in his own bathroom, and crawl into the bed he shared with Leo, but Leo said he'd likely have to stay another night for observation if no one recommended him for discharge before three.

The clock had just ticked over to seven fifteen, adding salt to the wound and making Cole freshly cranky.

Gran hung her coat on the hook behind the door and moved to stand next to the bed. "Cole, dear. You look rested."

Cole had done nothing but rest for a whole day. "I am ready to climb the walls." He'd shooed Leo out to eat and shower around three, because Leo looked worse than Cole felt. He hadn't returned yet, and Cole hadn't paid for the TV service to be turned on, and he was *bored*. "Sorry I missed the party. I know it's a big deal."

Gran made a dismissive noise. "Nonsense. There's always next year."

When Cole was a child, Gran had raised a huge fuss about ensuring he was there for every Samhain—no Halloween parties for him—so that made him raise his eyebrows, but he didn't comment.

"We were just lucky your young man was around," she went on. "Without his quick thinking… and if he hadn't known where to find your EpiPen!"

Something about that came out a little *too* casual. Cole sat up straighter, narrowing his eyes. *We were just lucky*, she said. "Were we really?"

Gran covered quickly, but Cole still caught it: a brief flash of guilt, or maybe panic. "Of course! Without Leo—"

"Are you telling me you didn't See any of this?" Cole broke in bravely. Because he didn't believe that for a second. When Ella was born, Gran had had the date circled on her calendar for months. Cousin Julie went into false labor twice, but Gran never wavered; the baby would come when she'd Seen it.

There—another chink in the armor. Gran clasped her hands in front of her. She'd always told Cole that crossing his arms made him look defensive. "Cole—"

But the sound of someone else at the door interrupted. Cole and his gran both swung their heads toward the newcomer, and for a second Cole almost felt bad for whoever it was; they probably looked like cobras about to strike. Then he took in the man standing in the doorway—dark-wash jeans, leather jacket, ebony skin, perfectly sculpted hair, cheekbones sharp enough to cut glass. He was handsome in a movie-star way, the kind of handsome

Cole would never be. Even the way he stood spoke of charisma. And under all the beauty and charm pulsed the unmistakable red aura of a vampire.

Roman.

"What are *you* doing here?" Gran and Roman said at the same time.

Roman answered first, maybe because Gran was just as terrifying to the undead. "Looking for Leo," he said in a rich baritone, cutting his eyes quickly to Cole. "James said I'd probably find him here."

Damn it, Jimmy, Cole thought. Also, did Roman have to have a beautiful voice on top of everything else? Talk about insult to injury.

"Well, as you can see, James was mistaken." Each clipped word dripped icicles. Gran wanted him *gone*.

All of a sudden exhaustion reared its head again. Cole just wanted the damn truth. "So," he said conversationally, "how do you two know each other?"

Gran turned sharply toward him, and there was no mistaking the stricken expression nor the guilt in her eyes. Cole had her dead to rights and she knew it.

Roman said smoothly, "I was a would-be client," and that cemented it.

Cole let suspicion harden his features, holding Gran's gaze. They were going to have this out here and now— but not with an audience. "I see," he said. "Roman—it is Roman, isn't it?"

Roman nodded. Even his *nod* radiated power and self-assurance.

"Roman, would you give my grandmother and me a moment? We have some important matters to discuss."

He probably could have argued. But maybe he sensed that Cole was on his side, because he simply inclined his head and took a step back, half closing the door behind him.

Cole very deliberately did not cross his arms. *He* wasn't on the defensive here. "Why did you do it?" he asked quietly. "What could you possibly gain from cursing Leo?" He didn't want to believe she'd done it, but what else was he supposed to think?

Gran's tone when she answered was just as frigid as it had been when she spoke to Roman. "I don't have to explain myself—"

"I think you do," Cole interrupted. "I think you do, Gran, because this level of petty curse on a man you didn't even know is skirting pretty close to gray magic. And you always told me that was wrong, and that it would knock the universe out of balance. So I think you better explain what you were doing."

"You don't understand." Now that cold refusal had failed, Gran turned pleading. "Cole, some things, a Seer just knows. Sometimes we have to act."

"To do *what*?" Cole half shouted. Someone in the hallway might overhear, but he was beyond caring. "What could cursing Leo possibly accomplish?"

"Saving your life!" Gran shouted back. "What happened yesterday, I Saw it when you were eight years old, before your mother ever moved away! I saw it a hundred different ways—I saw you die in Florida, in Tuscany, in Baha. I fought like hell to keep you here because I knew if I didn't, if I didn't find the right man, if I didn't make sure he was there, *you were going to die*."

For a second Cole stared at her, incredulous, imagining the weight of that knowledge. Then a wave of ice washed over him, receding with the last of his sympathy—and his patience. "So, what? Instead of warning me to be extra careful around chocolate on

Halloween, you...." Roman had said he was a would-be client. "Roman came to you to ask your price for a revenge hex," he guessed, and Gran's miniscule flinch let him know he'd guessed right. "He must have brought a picture and you saw. You knew it was the man from your vision. So you cursed him."

"I didn't officially ask her to go through with it!" Roman said loudly from the other side of the door. "In case you're wondering why I'm pissed!"

"Shut up!" Cole and Gran chorused.

But Cole wasn't done. "You cursed him just as Roman had suggested—so that he wouldn't be able to act on any of his feelings." His stomach twisted. "You must have known that eventually he would come to me."

After all, Cole was the best cursebreaker in Southwestern Ontario.

This time Gran said nothing in self-defense. To Cole, she might as well have signed a confession.

"You manipulated us," he said, his heart sinking. "You played us from the very beginning. The whole thing was a setup." So much for free will.

"How could you?" he whispered, his voice breaking. "How could you do that to me?"

Gran took one faltering step toward him. "I was trying to protect you. I *love* you. I couldn't stand it if—"

"If I got hurt?" Cole filled in venomously. "Because guess what, Gran? I *am* hurt." Not completely true. He was devastated. He and Leo had built their life on what he'd thought was a solid foundation. Now he discovered it was made of sand. "God, and even that wasn't enough, was it? Setting us up? No, you had to go further and—you sent those flowers to Leo with that enchanted vase so you could *scry him*, and then you stole the florist's memories—"

Did she even realize she'd crossed an elf? Had she been so consumed by her quest that she didn't care?

"I had to make sure!" Gran said, wringing her hands now. "I couldn't take any chances!"

Cole laughed hollowly, sinking back against his pillows. "Do you know what the funny thing is, Gran?" His eyes wanted to close with grief and exhaustion, but he needed to see her face when she realized the truth. "I never would have come into contact with those hazelnuts if it weren't for Leo. He's the one who asked if he could invite Amy along. I almost died because *you interfered*."

It happened as if in slow motion. Gran's mouth fell open, and her eyes went wide. Then realization overwhelmed the shock and her expression crumpled, the lines on her face deepening and her chin caving in. She raised a hand to her mouth. "What have I done?"

Watching the impact of his words, Cole expected to feel a grim satisfaction, a stinging balm over his own wounds.

Instead he felt immeasurably worse.

"Gran," he said helplessly, his eyes burning. "You can't—you can't ever do that to anyone again."

Gran nodded, wordless, face dripping with tears.

"Okay," Cole said. His voice cracked. "I'm really mad at you and I think you understand why. But now I need a hug."

She shuffled to the bed and put her arms around his shoulders. He wrapped his around her waist, and they both pretended the other wasn't crying. Then they pulled away, Gran dabbing her eyes with a handkerchief, Cole wiping his on the neck of his hospital gown.

Knock knock knock.

Cole looked up, sharp words for Roman ready on his tongue, only to see Leo standing in the doorway, expression serious.

No. Oh no. Cole's heart had been in his stomach; now it sank to his knees.

"Irene, I'd like to speak to Cole privately, please."

Gran shot Cole another stricken look but nodded wordlessly and walked toward the door, still dabbing at her eyes.

"There's coffee at the nurses' station," Leo murmured as she passed him. "Not as good as your tea, but they'll give you a cup if you tell them I sent you."

Gran bit her lip, as though she could not bear to receive kindness from someone she'd been so callous to, and then she nodded again and left.

When Leo closed the door, it clicked definitively. Cole thought about that sunny September day when Leo had walked into his candy shop and thought it was fitting; their time together had begun with a door opening, and now this one had closed.

"Roman put the doll in my bed," Leo said conversationally, surprising him. "Apparently I should have locked my windows. Did you know he could turn into a bat?"

Cole shook his head, scrambling for his conversational bearings. "Uh," he said. "No. I didn't know that."

"Well, that makes two of us." Leo shook his head. "Apparently he felt bad for letting his pride get the better of him and turning a witch on me, and tried to counter the spell."

Of course he had. All this, and Cole didn't even have the simple comfort of Leo's ex being an asshole. "So that's it, then," he said. "Mystery solved."

"Yeah. And Roman says he's got Kyle in the equivalent of vampire therapy to cope with the fact that he's gonna have acne for like two hundred years, so we can stop worrying about Jimmy too."

Cole dug for a smile and mustered one that felt like wax on his face. "Great." He took a breath and swallowed. "Look, you didn't sign up for any of this, and it's not fair to you. If you want to just—forget this ever happened, I understand. I can… we can make that happen." At least Cole could go on knowing they hadn't fucked up Leo's life for good, even if his own heart broke in the process.

Leo stared at him as though he'd grown a second head. "No, I don't want—are you offering to *Eternal Sunshine* me?"

Cole's mouth dropped open in surprise. "Technically I'm offering to have Gran do it," he said by rote. "Or Kate, if you never want to speak to Gran again, which I wouldn't blame you for."

For another handful of seconds Leo didn't say anything, didn't move. Then he shook his head and asked, "What is *wrong* with you? I know you didn't hit your head when you fell."

This time Cole couldn't find any words to fill the hole of his mouth.

Apparently he didn't need to; Leo continued on, undaunted. "What, you think that my feelings for you aren't real because your grandmother manipulated us into *spending time together*?" He scoffed. "I've spent a lot more time with a lot of other people, Cole. I roomed with the same guy for three years in university and I didn't fall in love with *him*."

Cole realized he was still searching for a rebuttal, then realized that was stupid. "So you're…."

"Well, I'm not exactly pleased to be part of a weird morality lesson on self-fulfilling prophecies." He took Cole's hand in both of his. "It's a little strange to realize that someone set us up on a really underhanded, extended blind date."

At that, Cole managed a real smile, though it felt tenuous. Hope bloomed in his chest. "A blind date that could only end with true love's kiss," he admitted. His heart was in his throat now.

Leo inched closer. "Well, I'm not going to argue with the results."

"Oh," Cole said, his whole body filling with relief. "Okay." He paused. "Same."

Leo laughed softly, leaning his head against Cole's. Cole closed his eyes and let warmth and contentment seep into his bones. "God, what a day. I could use one of those lemon fizzies."

"I've got a better idea," Cole murmured, tilting his head. After all, true love's kiss had its own kind of magic.

Coming in September 2018

Dreamspun Beyond #27
Somebody to Die For by Kris T. Bethke

Dying is easy. New love is terrifying.

Avery Wagner quit ghostwalking when he lost his beloved anchor to cancer. Now teaching others who have the ability, he's beginning to live again—but he's not looking for another lover, not now, maybe not ever.

But then he meets Jameson… younger, talented, dedicated, almost perfect, even though his mouth sometimes opens ahead of his brain. And Jameson wants Avery desperately, though he'll settle for friendship if he can't have more.

When an emergency demands they work together in the field, Avery discovers just how perfect Jameson is. But he had a perfect love once before, and he's scared to even consider that he might have a chance at another. Can he trust Jameson with his newly healing heart?

Dreamspun Beyond #28
Hiding in Plain Sight by Bru Baker

Happily ever after is right under their noses.

Harris has been keeping a big secret for years—his unrequited mate bond with his best friend, Jackson. He's convinced himself that having Jackson in his life is enough. That, and his work at Camp H.O.W.L., keeps him going.

Things get complicated when Jackson applies for a high-ranking Tribunal job in New York City—far from Camp H.O.W.L. The position requires he relinquish all Pack bonds… and that's when his wolf decides to choose a mate. Suddenly Jackson sees his best friend in a sizzling new light.

Their chemistry is through the roof, but they're setting themselves up for broken hearts—and broken bonds—if Jackson can't figure out a way to balance his career and the love that's just been waiting for him to take notice.

Love Always Finds a Way

REAMSPUN BEYOND

Subscription Service

Love eBooks?

Our monthly subscription service
gives you two eBooks per month for
one low price. Each month's titles
will be automatically delivered
to your Dreamspinner Bookshelf
on their release dates.

Prefer print?

Receive two paperbacks per month!
Both books ship on the 1st of the
month, giving you *exclusive* early
access! As a bonus, you'll receive
both eBooks on their release dates!

Visit
www.dreamspinnerpress.com
for more info or to sign up now!

FOR MORE OF THE BEST GAY ROMANCE

DREAMSPINNER
PRESS
dreamspinnerpress.com